I0687755

The Oxley Crossing Romances
Book 6

The Making of Joey Lambert

LENA WEST

Australian Rural Romance

Gymea Publishing

Published by Gymea Publishing

https://www.facebook.com/LenaWestAuthor/

www.lenawestauthor.com

ISBN-978-0-6482671-8-8

Disclaimer

This story is a work of **FICTION**.

Please remember that what works for Sienna in this story is purely **FICTIONAL**. Not to be confused with advice from a professional therapist. That is not what I am. I am merely a novelist whose characters and their actions spring from my imagination.

Names, characters, places and incidents are also the product of the author's imagination and are used fictitiously. Any resemblance to events, locales or actual persons, living or dead, is entirely coincidental.

Some actual locations may be referenced in passing.

Table of Contents

Here is Your Preview of

THE MAKING OF JOEY LAMBERT

Dedication

This novel is dedicated to Owen. I hope he knows his mother will always love him.

1

"Stop! Gwyneth, stop!"

Hearing the shouting, Joey Lambert, strolling out from Pete Hackett's hardware store, swung round. His heart chilling, he saw a young girl dashing after a soccer ball which was rolling out onto Bridge Street, the main east/west highway running through the centre of Oxley Crossing. His heart momentarily stalled, but not his feet.

Closer than the woman doing all the shouting, he instinctively raced forward, grabbing a fistful of the girl's shirt a split second before she ran into the path of an oncoming semi-trailer. The driver blasted his horn, and gave a thumbs up to Joey as he roared by. Panting, Joey returned the friendly gesture.

"My ball!" wailed the girl as she was hauled back onto the footpath and released.

"Gwynna! You nearly got skittled by that truck. Your ball's not that important."

Flinging herself to her knees, the petite, blonde woman clutched the girl, Gwyneth, tightly against her chest, looking gratefully up, way up, into Joey's chocolate-brown eyes, her own brimming with tears.

"Thank you."

Her voice shook, and she sucked in a deep breath before continuing. "Thank you so much. Gwynna mightn't realise how narrow an escape she had, but I do."

A brief, radiant smile bloomed as she stood, tilting her head to look up at her daughter's saviour. Almost every man stood head and shoulders above her diminutive one hundred and fifty-seven centimetres, although on closer inspection, she calculated her lanky hero stood only a smidgen above the male average. Still, he was tall enough from where she stood. Tall, but not in the least overpowering.

Her smile placed a hook in Joey's heart which nothing would ever dislodge. Catching glimpses of her around town, he'd thought she was shy, only there was not a smidgen of shyness in that smile. Nothing of flirtation either. Joey felt she'd seen to the heart of him; and honestly liked what she'd seen. Stunned, he struggled to find his voice. It came out husky. Uttering nothing, when he longed to say something memorable.

"My pleasure, Ma'am."

Polite, too. Like an old-fashioned cowboy.

Sienna felt an hysterical giggle bubbling up inside her chest. Recognising it for what it was, reaction to the fright Gwynna had given her, she swallowed it back down, letting another brief smile take its place.

Joey blushed to the roots of the mop of untidy brown curls riding his shoulders. Even his sprinkling of freckles, those not hidden beneath a bushy beard, took on a rosy glow. He'd noticed this pretty young woman several times since the New Year long weekend. Noticed, male antenna instantly alert.

He'd wondered if she'd be in town long enough to warrant the effort of scheming an 'accidental' meeting to get up close and personal.

Mission accomplished, with no scheming required.

The warmth heating his face moved south, warming him all the way to his toes. And important parts of his anatomy in between.

A younger, mirror image of the woman, the child constantly at her side every time he'd glimpsed her, had been all that held him back from approaching her.

Her daughter?

Married women were way off limits to his way of thinking. Because of the child, Joey had assumed she was married, but now, seeing them up close, he wondered. Although women's ages could be deceptive, Sienna looked a bit on the young side to have a kid this old. Seven or eight, he estimated roughly. About the age of his youngest sister.

He ran a nervous hand through his hair, then impulsively offered it to her, a surreptitious glance having yielded the encouraging sight of a completely bare left hand.

Maybe the kid was her sister? If so, it was up to him to make the most of this heaven-sent opportunity. Joey tendered his best wide, friendly smile along with his hand.

"Couldn't just stand there and watch your kiddie get hit. Joey Lambert, Ma'am. Glad I could be of service."

Hazel eyes skittered away from his, as if finding the cracks in the pavement more interesting. Straight white teeth bit her bottom lip, as the young woman hesitated before taking Joey's hand.

Hesitated so long, he wondered indignantly if she thought the contact might contaminate her.

As she shook hands, she flashed a quick upward glance, smiling politely with none of the radiance of her earlier smiles.

"Sienna Smith. Pleased to meet you Joey. And this is my daughter, Gwyneth Smith."

Question answered. Her daughter. Joey wasn't sure how he felt about that. He'd never had a girlfriend who had a kid in tow. *Girlfriend? Jumping the gun there, Lambert. Still, that bare ring finger …*

But he was getting ahead of himself, he realised. Just because he was looking, didn't mean … And he still didn't know if she was a free agent, married, or not.

He gave a mental shrug.

Sienna gave her daughter a gentle nudge to remind her of her manners.

"Thank you for saving me, Mr Lambert."

"You've got pretty names, you and your Mum."

Self-conscious with hero status, Joey sought to change the subject. And maybe elicit another crumb or two of information.

"Do you think so? Grandma says when your name is Smith, you need something a bit different to 'stinguish you from all the other Smiths."

"Sounds like your Grandma knows a thing or two."

Joey was still sufficiently curious, make that interested, to fish for more information. Sienna Smith was the prettiest girl he'd seen in quite a while. Hope flared in his breast thinking she might be available after all.

"Do you live here in Oxley Crossing, Gwynna?"

Questioning the child was a risk that had Joey holding his breath. Especially when out of the corner of his eye, he saw Sienna frown at her daughter. When she made no move to put a stop to the conversation, he breathed a little easier.

"Yes, Mr Lambert." Gwyneth was as free with her smiles as Sienna was parsimonious. "Mummy's a teacher, and Oxley Crossing is her very first school. She's going to start work as soon as the holidays are over."

Joey's heart sank again. He was beginning to feel a yo-yo had taken up residence in his chest.

'Teacher' meant a university education. From time to time he'd flirted unsuccessfully with other young teachers doing their country service in The Crossing. He did an honest day's work for an honest day's pay, and found it offensive when a pretty girl talked down to him as if a mere yard hand at the sawmill was beneath her.

As if his lack of education denoted a lack of intelligence.

Not academically inclined, and with five younger siblings to be provided for, his parents would have been stretched to the limit if he'd chosen to go to uni. Instead, he'd opted to take the best job he could get at the time. But, ever the optimist, he thought maybe this girl would be different. Maybe she'd realise he wasn't stupid. He'd see.

"So, Gwynna, is your daddy coming to live in The Crossing too?"

He was really pushing his luck now, but he simply had to know whether Sienna Smith was spoken for.

Or not.

"I don't have a daddy," Gwynna replied as if it was a matter of absolutely no importance. "It's just Mummy and me."

Interrupting Joey's musings, Gwyneth turned to her mother.

"Mummy, can I go and get my ball, now? I can see it in the gutter across the road."

"I'll get it," Joey volunteered, giving a mental air-pump.

Free! Well, except for the kid. And, with his pack of younger siblings, he was used to kids.

Returning, ball in hand, he pushed his luck a little further. After all, nothing ventured, nothing gained. Or should that be faint heart never won fair maid?

I need to get a grip, he thought, feeling a wee bit light-headed.

"How about joining me for a coffee at Tan's?"

Joey gestured to the bakery-café across from where they stood.

This time it was Sienna, eyes cast down to the pavement once more, who blushed.

Shy?

Joey's eyes opened wide. He hadn't realised shy girls still existed. He was used to the girls he'd grown up with. Country girls who were as assertive as the blokes. His pulse rate accelerated slightly.

"I'd like to Joey. I really would." Sienna flashed him another of those split-second smiles, then lowered her eyes again. "Only, I've got an appointment to get my hair trimmed. I'll be late if we don't get going."

"Okay." His heart sank. Was this a polite brush-off? He decided to give Sienna Smith the benefit of the doubt. "Say hello to Thea and the girls for me," he said, adding optimistically, "Can we take a raincheck on the coffee?"

Thea and the girls?

Was this unassuming young man really a wolf in sheep's clothing? A momentary panic almost sent her fleeing until Sienna recalled how much she owed him.

"That would be good. Bye Joey, and thanks again for saving my girl." She gave a little wave and, taking Gwyneth's hand, quickly disappeared down the street.

"Bye Mr Lambert," Gwyneth called. "Thanks for bringing my ball back."

Joey stood staring after them for a moment, then giving himself a mental shake, headed off in the opposite direction, back to the tiny flat he rented behind Bill Whitman's place.

He'd pulled a swifty there, beating out a couple of other blokes looking for accommodation. The idea of continuing to share the sleepout at the farm with his younger brothers had been incentive enough to urge him to approach Hazel Whitman as soon as her son, Robert, won the byelection and moved to Canberra, vacating the flat behind his parents' house.

Whistling as he walked, he slowed to a halt in front of the library. Nodding to himself, he pushed open the door and strolled in. He'd fallen into a rut, he thought, and it was high time he climbed out of it.

"Hi Aunt Eddie," he called, following the greeting up with a smacking kiss on the lips. Edith Patterson, the librarian, blushed and tittered.

"You and your nonsense, Joey Lambert," she bridled. "How can I help you?"

"With what you're best at, Eddie. Advice and information. With all the recent layoffs at sawmills up and down the country, I've been thinking it'd be a wise move to look for another job. Maybe acquire a few decent qualifications along the way."

"Wonderful, Joey. I told you years ago that's what you ought to do."

"You did. I listened, and here I am Aunt Eddie. Better late than never, don't you think?"

My decision has nothing to do with impressing Sienna Smith, Joey assured himself. *Nothing at all. Quite simply, the timing is right. Perfect, in fact, with the academic year starting at the end of January. Straight after Australia Day.*

I'll stick with it, too, he silently vowed.

Eddie's never given up on me, so I'll do it for her as well as myself.

She wasn't really his aunt, but she'd taken him under her wing a long time ago when he'd been the victim of the school bully, and ever since she'd been his honorary aunt.

Smiling delightedly, Eddie patted him on the should.

"Then let's go into my office and discuss your options over a coffee. Sue," Eddie called to her assistant, "hold the fort for me, will you Dear."

2

"Say hello to Thea and the girls for me," Joey Lambert had said, so, finding herself the recipient of the services of Thea Marten, proprietor of the salon, Sienna did just that.

Thea had immediately impressed her as a woman with a ton of common sense, especially valuable as she didn't quite trust her own judgement where men were concerned, and reckoned Thea's reaction would tell her a lot about the kind of man Joey Lambert really was. In her, admittedly limited, experience, hairdressers knew all the local gossip. Not that she was remotely interested in him in *that* way. That would be absurd, considering ... But she had liked him. As a friend. And wasn't making new friends a large part of her reason for accepting a teaching position in Oxley Crossing?

"Joey?" Thea laughed. "You've been in town less than a fortnight and you've already got the boys chasing after you," she teased.

With difficulty Sienna controlled her instinctive shudder. She didn't want to accidently end up with a gap cut into her chic, shoulder-length new hairstyle.

"I've got a lot of time for Joey," Thea continued, her attention mostly concentrated on Sienna's hair. "You'll hear some people write him off as a bit of a galah, what with his clowning around, but underneath it he's solid as a rock. Totally reliable."

"If you're looking for character references anytime, Sienna," Lisa Tan, Thea's apprentice chimed in from where she was sweeping up hair clippings, "you ought to have a chat with Eddie Patterson. There's nothing she doesn't know about what goes on in Oxley Crossing."

"Eddie hangs out in the library when she's not poking her nose into someone else's business." Vera Nichols, hanging up the phone from making an appointment, added her somewhat sour mite to the conversation.

"Don't be mean, Vera, just because she told your Jimmy to shape up or he'd end up in trouble." Petite Lisa didn't hesitate to stand up to Vera who'd have made two of her. "Eddie was spot-on. You know she was, and wasn't she the first to congratulate him when he did get his act together?"

"Peace, ladies." Thea, blow-drying Sienna's hair, intervened. "Lisa's right, though, Sienna. If you've got any questions about The Crossing or its inhabitants, Eddie's your go-to woman. And if it's advice you need, she's tight as an oyster. No fear of her blabbing private stuff around town. Although, mind you, anything else is fair game. She does like to be first with the latest. There, all finished. How do you like it?"

She held a mirror up so Sienna could view her hair, front and back.

"Perfect. It's just what I hoped for, Thea. My old style was okay, but a bit childish."

She fluffed her loose, shorter hair, enjoying the feel of it.

"This gives me a little bit of much-needed gravitas. I don't want the parents to write me off as wet behind the ears, even if I am new to the job."

A few minutes later, Lisa and Vera were both busy with clients who'd just arrived. Gwyneth had taken her mother's place in Thea's chair, chatting away, nineteen-to-the-dozen in her usual open, innocent manner, telling the hair stylist about her mother's new job, and how much she, Gwynna, was looking forward to meeting the local kids and making new friends.

"Will you be living in the school flats?" Thea directed her question to Sienna, referring to the block of government flats built to house itinerant incomers employed at the school, hospital and council. Most of these people kept to themselves, having little to do with the locals.

"No. There were no vacancies, for which I'm glad, having seen them. They're all so close to each other. I'm really lucky. I signed the lease this last week on a lovely house in Nymboida Street. Gwynna and I gave it a once over this morning. Just in time," she laughed. "My furniture arrives tomorrow afternoon."

What she didn't say was that the furniture was all brand new. A whole house package deal from a nationwide chain of stores. She didn't think it would add to her consequence for it to be known that until a bit over a week ago she'd still lived at home with her parents. She and Gwynna.

The change was as much for Gwynna's sake as her own. Her parents had been wonderful, except they kept the two of them cotton-woolled and isolated from the outside world.

She didn't blame her parents for being over-protective, but it was past time she stood on her own two feet. Past time Gwynna enjoyed the freedom other kids took for granted. Sienna crossed her fingers, hoping that in choosing the small country town of Oxley Crossing she'd made the right choice.

"Our new house is painted blue," Gwynna added. "That's my favourite colour. There's a lovely garden, too, and Mum says I can have a play-house in the back yard. I wish I had a friend to play with, though."

"Blue house in Nymboida Street? Number 24, is it?"

"That's right? How did you guess?" Gwynna asked, impressed by Thea's omniscience.

"Small town. I was friends with the people who used to live there. They bought a place of their own out of town. And Sienna?" Thea turned her attention from child to mother. "You heard us talking about Eddie Patterson?" Sienna nodded. "She's your new next-door neighbour, at number 22. Don't be put off by Vera, I'm sure you'll find Eddie and Mike the perfect neighbours. While I'm at it, organising your lives, Lisa," she called to the young apprentice, "Why don't you send that young cousin of yours round to say hello to Gwynna. They're about the same age, and I'm sure Molly's at a loose end till school goes back."

Then, with Gwynna's hair finished, the Smiths were soon on their way.

~~~~~

"Shall we go to the library and borrow some books?"

Sienna had an ulterior motive for her suggestion.
~~~~~

Intrigued by what she'd heard, she wanted to catch a glimpse of her new neighbour. She'd judge the woman for herself, but Thea's endorsement predisposed her to look favourably on her.

"Yes please, Mum!" Gwynna gave a little hop and skip, swinging off her mother's hand. "I've read everything I got for Christmas over and over. Do you think they'll have any Alison Lester stories here?"

"Should have, but it's only a small town, so don't be disappointed if the library isn't what you're used to."

"We're not a big library," the woman whose badge simply read 'Sue', said, repeating Sienna's caution a few minutes later, "but we're affiliated with a huge library network across the whole region. You can order books online or through us, and they'll be sent here for you to pick up. A bit slower than you're used to, perhaps, but there's nothing we don't have access to."

"Sounds wonderful. Where do I sign?"

Sue laughed, fishing an application form out of the draw of her desk. "Why don't you fill this out while Gwynna picks out some books to take with her."

Handing back the completed form, Sienna looked up as a door behind the desk opened. A kindly looking older lady came out, talking over her shoulder to … -Sienna gulped, feeling her face flame – Joey Lambert.

"Hey Eddie," Sue looked up from checking Sienna's application. "You'll never guess who this is. Come and meet your new next-door neighbour. Sienna Smith, meet Eddie Patterson. Joey Lambert, too," she added.

"Sienna and I have already met. Hi again, Sienna." Joey could have kicked himself. Here he was, being given another chance to impress, and all he could come up with was a feeble greeting.

Keen eyes behind Dame Edna Everage style glasses shrewdly observed the self-conscious body language of the two young people. Taking pity on them, Eddie stepped forward to welcome her new neighbour.

"Are you the new teacher moving into number 24?"

"That's right. Sienna Smith, and my daughter, Gwyneth. Gwynna," she amended as the girl reappeared with several books clutched in her hands.

"We're going to live in the blue house," Gwynna informed Eddie, politely offering her hand. "Hello Mr Lambert. Where do you live?"

Sue and Eddie both chuckled. Joey looked embarrassed.

"Just across the street," he mumbled. "Behind the Whitman's house. Number 29."

The formalities of book borrowing completed, Sienna ushered Gwynna out the door to discover Joey Lambert loitering on the street outside.

"I wanted to tell you how much I like the new hairstyle," he said, coming to stand beside her, "only not in front of Eddie. She's the world's biggest romantic. Just let her suspect a guy likes a girl and next thing she's in full match-maker mode. Not that I don't like you, Sienna, because I do. Eddie too, only ..."

Confusing himself, he blushed, fading off. Uncertain how Sienna was taking his rambling on.

Kind. Pushy. A busy-body. Gossip. Trustworthy confidant. Now match-maker. I might not know much about anybody else, but I'm sure getting to know a lot about my new neighbour, Eddie Patterson.

Sienna glanced up into Joey's face, noting the blush. *About my other new neighbour, too,* she thought, embarrassed to feel her own cheeks heating under his intent gaze.

She wasn't usually comfortable around men. Young men especially, but, shy and self-effacing, Joey Lambert wasn't setting off any warning bells. Before she could change her mind, Sienna gulped a lungful of air and plunged right in.

"Joey, you asked earlier for a raincheck on coffee. Do you have time to join Gwynna and I now?"

Her temerity almost terrified Sienna into turning tail and running for cover, but she held her ground. Just. She'd come to Oxley Crossing to make a new start. To live a normal life, and that included a normal social life. Who better to try her new wings with than Joey Lambert who didn't scare her one little bit?

"Sure thing."

Wild horses couldn't have kept Joey from accepting Sienna's unexpected invitation. He'd thought she wasn't interested, but maybe she was.

~~~~~

Joey had insisted coffee was his treat, as he'd been the first to issue the invitation, so Sienna gracefully acceded, going to sit with Gwynna at a table in the shady outdoor seating area while he went to place their order.
~~~~~

"I know you said no cakes, but I ordered some of Geoff Tan's little glazed fruit and custard tarts," Joey said, slipping into his seat next to Sienna. "He's a terrific baker, and they're only tiny. You'll like them."

While they waited, Joey answered their questions about Oxley Crossing and its denizens. Forgetting to feel self-conscious on such safe ground, Joey surprised Sienna with his ready wit. Some of his descriptions of people cut close to the bone, but not, she realised, unkindly.

The more time she spent in his company, the easier she felt.

"Here you are. Two coffees, a milkshake and fruit tarts. Who are your friends, Joey?"

"Elizabeth!" surprised, Joey looked up. Engrossed in his conversation with Sienna, he hadn't seen her crossing the courtyard to their table.

"Elizabeth Tan, Sienna and Gwynna Smith," he introduced them to each other. "Sienna is a new teacher down at the school," he added, knowing Elizabeth would never be satisfied with merely being told their names. He was about to add more when she interrupted him.

"I've heard about you, Sienna!" she exclaimed. "My husband's cousin, Lisa, works for Thea in the salon. She rang to tell me all about you." Smiling, Elizabeth then addressed herself exclusively to Gwynna.

"Lisa said you'd like to make some new friends, Gwynna. Is that right?" You come in here tomorrow morning and my little girl, Molly, will be here. Her best friend moved away and she's lonely too. You can be friends with her."

With that, Elizabeth whisked herself back inside leaving Sienna somewhat bemused and Gwynna chattering on about what she and Molly would do together tomorrow.

"Elizabeth's pure gold," Joey offered, seeing she'd been taken aback by the older woman's forthright manner. "Her kids are okay too. Gwynna and Molly will probably be in the same class, so it'll be nice for them to get to know each other before school starts."

So that's us all fixed up.

Sienna wasn't sure how she felt. Oxley Crossing seemed to have opened its arms wide and wrapped herself and Gwynna up in a big welcoming embrace.

On the whole, although she'd not experienced anything like it before, she thought it was probably a good thing.

3

"So that's about it, Mum." As promised, Sienna was making her daily phone call to her mother after dinner that evening. "We got the house ready this morning, and the furniture we ordered in Tamworth last week will be delivered tomorrow afternoon. Marge and Phil Morris have made us very comfortable, but it will be really good to move out of the hotel into our own home."

"Did I tell you it's a blue house, Grandma?" Sienna had put the phone on speaker to allow Gwynna to share the call. "The nice lady from the library lives next door, and Joey Lambert lives across the street."

"Joey Lambert? Have you found a little playmate, Gwyn darling?"

"Nooo Grandma," Gwynna laughed.

Sienna's heart sank. She'd hoped to escape being put through the third degree about her new acquaintance. Friend, she corrected herself. Joey was a friend, but one she'd prefer Gwynna hadn't mentioned so soon. Her mother was bound to worry.

"Joey is a grown-up, Grandma. He saved my life this arvo when a huge truck nearly ran over me."

Joy Smith's horrified gasp was clearly audible over the phone.

"It's okay, Mum," Sienna rushed to reassure her. "She's not hurt at all. It wasn't as close as Gwynna made it sound, but she does need to polish up her street skills."

"So, Sienna, who was this man who rescued her?" Reassured of her granddaughter's continued good health, Joy returned to her original question.

"He's a local, Mum. Works up at the sawmill. We were really lucky he was passing by at exactly the right time." She tried to divert her mother's attention away from Joey, but knew it would be futile.

"If he's got a job, how come he was down the street in the middle of the afternoon?"

Sienna rolled her eyes. Trust her mother to want to know everything.

"The sawmill starts early and finishes early," she explained. Forestalling her mother's next question, she went on. "He's about my age, maybe a year or two older. Not particularly impressive, but quite pleasant." She felt a bit disloyal dissing Joey who'd been nothing but kind, but if it got her mother off her back … Her conscience forced her to add, "At least four different people have all given him their stamp of approval."

"Have you been asking about him?" Her mother sounded appalled.

"Didn't have to," Sienna laughed.

'Gwynna's been broadcasting her adventure far and wide. To the hairdressers, the librarians, and at dinner to Marge Morris, the publican's wife. They all said he's a decent bloke."

"Will you be seeing this young man again?"

"Undoubtedly, Mum. It's a small town, and as Gwynna said, he lives across the street. But if you mean seeing, as in 'seeing', not much likelihood of that, is there? I don't date, remember?"

Sienna couldn't help the tinge of bitterness which even she heard in her voice.

"Oh, Darling, I'm so sorry to have reminded you. Only, you will be careful, won't you? Your father and I can't help being worried sick with you both so far away."

Using the excuse of Gwynna's bedtime, Sienna wound up the conversation and tucked her daughter in, turning out the light and going to sit on the veranda. The questions her mother had asked about Joey had unsettled her. Saddened her.

If I was a normal girl, I bet I would go out with him. If he asked.

It wasn't fair. It just wasn't.

~~~~~

"C'mon Mum, hurry up. She'll think I'm not coming."

"Okay. Slow down, Gwynna. It's only just round the corner."

Sienna yawned for the fifth time since breakfast. Last night she'd tossed and turned and had vivid, uncomfortable dreams. Woken far too early by Gwynna rattling on about whether she'd like Molly Tan, and whether Molly would like her, it had been all Sienna could do not to yell at her daughter to be quiet.
~~~~~

She'd tried burying her head under the pillow, but, yielding to the inevitable, she'd dragged herself off to the shower then set about packing their cases ready to check out after breakfast.

Tonight we sleep in our own beds. In our own house. The first time I've ever been completely alone. Except for Gwynna, of course.

Their stay in the historic *Victoria Inn* didn't count. Not with the solid security of Marge and Phil Morris at the other end of the corridor.

A swarm of butterflies stirred in her tummy.

The move would be exciting, Sienna thought. And a little bit scary at the same time. There'd be no-one to come running if she woke up hearing strange noises in the night. No-one to hold her if the nightmares returned. She hadn't had one for years, but her disturbed night had reawakened her fears.

I'm not the kid with parents watching out for me. From now on, I'm the parent, she reminded herself. I need to toughen up a bit. For Gwynna's sake.

The huge responsibility her new life entailed almost had her jumping in white Subaru Forester her parents had bought her for Christmas and heading back to Sydney.

Back to Mum and Dad.

Back to being a prisoner of my fears.

Not what I want. I'm never going back to that. Gwynna deserves a normal life; and, so do I.

Sienna gulped, fingers curling into fists.

Consciously straightening them, she worked her way through the sequence of calming exercises her psychologist, Dr Gail Michaelson, had taught her. Still feeling nervous, she ran through them a second time.

Reminding herself how much she was looking forward to embarking on a new life, a normal life, where she'd be just like every other girl, she exited the bathroom and took Gwynna down to breakfast.

No-one watching would have seen through her bright, cheerful smiles as she chatted to Marge, to the butterflies still fluttering sickeningly in her stomach.

Breakfast over, the panic attack was also over, but it had left Sienna exhausted. Maybe Molly Tan, whom nobody had consulted, would refuse to play with Gwynna and they could come back and rest a while longer. No, that was mean of her, Sienna thought. She really hoped Gwynna would find a much-needed friend in Molly.

All my worrying for nothing.

The little girl sitting forlornly outside the bakery jumped to her feet, running to meet them as they approached the door.

"You must be Gwynna," she called. "I'm Molly. Have you come to play with me?"

"What do you want to play first, Molly?" Gwynna dispensed with unnecessary introductions and skipped to the more important issue.

"Why don't you two discuss that while I say hello to Molly's mother?"

Smiling, Sienna shook her head.

Totally engrossed in examining the collection of toys in Gwynna's backpack, she doubted either of the girls had heard a word she said.

"Molly has been that excited," Elizabeth said. "She woke me up early so we wouldn't be late."

"Gwynna too," Sienna laughed. Explaining how she had already checked out of the hotel, she asked if it would be alright to take Molly across Bridge Street to the park.

"Course it's okay. Molly loves the playground, but I don't let her go by herself. There are bad people out there in the world." A fact of life Sienna was only too aware of.

She and Gwynna had checked out the playground soon after arriving in The Crossing, only then the park had been full of teenagers mucking about in the cricket nets, and toddlers chasing balls around on the grass. No kids Gwynna's age, although the first-class equipment in the playground was definitely age-appropriate for her. She'd tried out the swings, slides and flying fox, but without someone to share it with she'd soon lost interest.

Today was different. Today Gwynna had a friend to share with.

Molly grabbed her own backpack loaded with little-girl essentials, and they were off, barely slowing down to let Sienna see them safely across the highway.

Settled on a park bench conveniently placed in the shade of an old peppercorn tree, Sienna felt surplus to requirements. Putting on her headphones, she tuned in to her favourite playlist, bopping in place while she kept her eyes on the girls.

It was almost as restful as another hour in bed would have been.

An hour later, she jerked awake with a start, her eyes going instantly to the swings where she'd last seen the girls. Not there! Her heart stopped! Then a familiar peal of laughter quelled incipient panic before it took hold. There they were! Over on the swing bridge between the climbing towers, along with two more little girls.

"Sienna Smith?"

Sienna looked up, thanking her stars she'd woken up before this young woman arrived. She looked enough like an older version of Molly for Sienna to be fairly certain they were closely related. An assumption proved correct when the newcomer plonked herself down beside her.

"Josie Tan," she said. "Moll's cousin and usual babysitter while I'm home from uni. Thanks for giving me a break."

Josie looked to be about her own age.

A new friend for me, too?

"What are you studying?" she asked, feeling her way.

"Dentistry. Following in my Dad's footsteps. Two years to go. I know you're a teacher. Is that what you always wanted to do, or did you fall into it by default?"

"I didn't 'fall into' teaching, but it was a fairly recent career choice," Sienna answered, careful not to give the wrong impression. She might have been late deciding, but she was fully committed.

"When Gwynna started preschool, I spent quite a bit of time there at first, dropping her off, and picking her up. Volunteering. Her teachers really impressed me, and I felt totally comfortable in the classrooms with little kids buzzing around."

Smiling at the memories invoked, she continued.

"I discovered how much I like working with children, especially the younger ones. Which is why I'm really happy Mrs Marsden has assigned me to the Kindergarten class."

Feeling a bit breathless at imparting so much information with barely a pause for breath, Sienna blushed faintly, wondering if she'd said too much. She really wasn't used to making casual conversation with strangers.

"Is Caro Marsden still head of the primary department? She taught me when I was in year six. Tell her hello from me when you see her next. She runs a tight ship."

That had been Sienna's impression, too. She'd found it comforting to know there'd be no nonsense in her workplace.

"Hey kids!" Yelling, Josie stood up and waved. In normal tones, she added to Sienna, "I've brought morning tea. Courtesy of Elizabeth."

She reached into the bag she'd put on the seat beside her, handing a take-away mug to Sienna. "Cappuccino. Same as you had yesterday." By then all four of the girls who'd been playing together had arrived.

"Gwynna, this is Molly's cousin Josie."

"Hello Josie. And Mum, this is Clarice and Estelle. They're twins."

"Well, you know," Sienna looked from one girl to the other, "I rather thought they might be. Hello girls. Which of you is Clarice and which one Estelle?"

"I'm Clarice," one of them shyly admitted.

"You can tell us apart because I've lost my front teeth and Clary hasn't yet," her sister chimed in.

"Okay brats," Josie took over. "Drinks and eats all round. Now scoot, so we grown-ups can talk. Don't forget to bin your rubbish," she instructed as the four children giggled and obeyed her instruction to scoot.

"Murphy twins," Josie said nodding after the girls. "Their parents are Oxley Crossing's worst losers. Both alcoholics. Half the time those poor kids and their older sibs are left roaming the streets unsupervised and with their belly-buttons sticking to their backbones. Maybe not so bad lately, since Sergeant Matthews stepped in and sicced Welfare onto them, but still, it's a damned shame. They're not bad kids, but the parents ... Don't let me get started."

Sienna frowned. She'd noticed the unkempt looking little girls were painfully thin, their clothes way more ragged than anything Gwynna owned. She felt righteous indignation steaming to a boil.

"Can't anyone do something?"

"We've all tried. Social services say the family should be kept together. That the parents love their kids. Hah! If they were mine and I loved them I'd get help to kick the booze and take proper care of them."

She saw Sienna was still frowning.

"Not even Eddie Patterson could do anything, and, believe me, Sienna, if Eddie can't fix it, it's beyond fixing. So now, the town quietly closes ranks and sees to it those poor little buggers don't starve. That's why, when I saw them playing with our two, I went back for extra supplies."

Oxley Crossing may look perfect on the surface, but I guess every Eden has its rotten apple.

It reminded Sienna how lucky she was. Her life wasn't perfect either, far from it; but she'd never been subjected to the kind of domestic abuse the Murphy children had to endure.

Sipping coffee with Josie in companionable silence, she was still thinking about plight of the Murphy children when her phone rang.

"What? Now? Okay. Okay, I'm on my way to meet you."

She looked apologetically at Josie.

"That was my delivery driver. He's ahead of schedule and will be here in ten minutes. I'll have to grab Gwynna and run. Will you be okay with Molly? She can come round to my house tomorrow, if you like, to make up for cutting this play-date short."

"Better than that, Sienna. I'll keep Gwynna with me for the afternoon. The last thing you need is to have a kid underfoot while you're unpacking. They can watch *Frozen*. Again." Josie rolled her eyes, grinning to show she didn't really mean it.

"Oh Josie, thank you. You're an angel."

A quick goodbye to Gwynna, and Sienna ran across the street to collect her car and drive round to Nymboida Street to receive her furniture delivery.

4

Her car parked out of the way a couple of doors up, Sienna raced up her steps and across the broad front veranda to unlock the door and catch it back to allow easy access for the delivery team. Ready with time to spare, she caught herself gazing across the street, squinting to make out the numbers. There. The pale grey and white house with the dark blue front door had a clearly discernible 29 on the mailbox.

Annoyed with herself, Sienna shook her head. She had better things to concern herself with than trying to catch a glimpse of Joey Lambert's tousled curls. Much better. Besides, it was hours too early for him to be home from work.

Her little lecture to herself didn't do much good, because, hours later, busily unpacking and arranging her new possessions with half an eye unconsciously patrolling the street outside, she felt her spirits drooping. Joey must have passed by when she wasn't looking. Part of her had been hoping he'd stop to look in; see how she was settling in. Or, greatly daring, she could give him a casual wave from the veranda. As a friend would.

But maybe he didn't care.

Maybe what she'd interpreted as friendly interest had been no more than politeness.

Maybe, during the shared coffee which had meant so much to her, he'd detected some not-normal quality in her behaviour and decided to keep out of her way in case she got the wrong idea. This supposition firmed into fact when the next week went by with not the tiniest, most fleeting glimpse of the man. Even Gwynna, not the most observant of children, had commented on Joey Lambert's elusiveness.

It wasn't as if she'd been hiding herself away, either. Most of her neighbours, bearing small gifts of flowers, homemade preserves and cuttings for her garden, had popped in to introduce themselves, staying for a cuppa on the veranda she'd furnished invitingly in tropical looking white cane. She'd even had a confidential chat with Eddie Patterson about the Murphy children who'd become frequent companions of Gwynna's.

"Just go on being kind to the children, dear," Eddie had advised. "Their situation isn't quite as bad as most people assume. Colin Murphy has grown children from his first marriage who keep a watchful eye on the family. I let Bridget know when she's needed." Unspoken had been the inference that she, Sienna, a stranger in town, might do more harm than good if she started making waves.

All the same, with Gwynna claiming the twins as friends, Sienna decided she, too, would keep a watchful eye on those children.

Putting her musings aside, she was annoyed to realise her 'watchful eye' was once again focused on the gate to number 29.

Toughen up, she ordered herself.

It's not the end of the world if one person decides they don't want to be friends after all. I've got more important things to do than moon about wishing for the impossible.

One good thing though, she thought, her lips curling into a wry smile, Joey's failure to follow up on their first meeting had set her mother's mind at rest. For several days, Joy had asked about him in their daily calls, but she hadn't mentioned him since Monday.

~~~~~

"Joey!"

At Gwynna's excited squeal, Sienna's head whipped round, her heart thudding. She'd been busy planting a border around the base of the bird bath near her front steps, and the sudden movement almost tumbled her onto her backside on the grass.

"Where have you been?" No polite holding back for Gwynna. When she had a question, she simply blurted it out.

"Hi girls." Joey's cheerful greeting, accompanied by his trademark broad grin, was aimed impartially at both Sienna and her daughter. "I've not been far, kiddo. Did you miss me?"

While his words were directed at Gwynna, he cast a hopeful glance in her mother's direction. He hoped Sienna had missed him, because he'd sure as Hell missed her. Every day for the last week he'd been itching to follow up on the promising start he'd made on getting to know her.

Rising to her feet and dusting her hands on the seat of her shorts as she came to the fence, Sienna's lips smiled, but her eyes didn't.
~~~~~

They held a wariness that had Joey's heart doing the yo-yo thing in his chest again. He rushed into an explanation of his absence before she could give him his marching orders.

"Dad's been laid up. Paul, my oldest brother still at home, is only sixteen, so after work I've been giving Mum a hand on the farm. Was easier to stay out there till Dad was back on his feet."

"You're a good son," Sienna said, annoyed to feel a guilty flush heating her cheeks. He hadn't been avoiding her. She had nothing to do with his absence.

How vain, to think I did. Would a normal girl have jumped to that conclusion? She doubted it. Normal girls knew where they stood.

An impulse to make amends overtook her.

"Come on in," she invited. "We were getting tired of gardening, and you've given us a perfect excuse to down tools."

No second invitation required. Joey was through the gate before Sienna finished speaking, his eagerness rousing the butterflies which were long-term permanent residents in her stomach.

"Sit down." She waved at the chairs on the shady veranda. "I'll fetch some iced tea." Hospitality only went so far. No-one, no male that was, was going to be invited across her threshold, no matter how innocuous he seemed. The veranda was it.

Gwynna was only too happy to entertain their visitor until her mother returned with a tray of glasses, the jug of pomegranate iced tea she'd made that morning and a plate of choc-chip biscuits that she'd left cooling on the rack.

Joey, who'd been watching the door, sprang to his feet, holding it open for her when she returned, thereby earning one of Sienna's radiant smiles.

He earned another a few minutes later.

"Seriously good biscuits, Sienna," he complimented her, licking the last crumbs of a second hastily demolished biscuit from his lips.

"I like baking." She blushed at the mild compliment. "I've been stocking the tins, ready for school lunches next week."

"So, are you all settled in? If Mum hadn't needed me, I'd have offered you a hand."

Sienna thanked him, but except for putting in a few more drought-hardy plants in the garden, which she didn't bother to mention, she was all set.

"What about you, Shortstuff? Are you ready for school?"

To Sienna's delight, Joey continued to include Gwynna in the conversation.

Which allowed her to sit back, letting their chatter flow over her as Gwynna enthusiastically brought Joey up-to-date about her friendships with Molly, Clarice and Estelle. When he directed the conversation back to Sienna, she was taken by surprise.

"It's Australia Day on Sunday, Sienna. Have you heard about the family picnic at Rainbow Falls during the afternoon?"

"Oh, yes. It sounds like fun. I was so glad when the Tans invited us to join them. It's always nicer to go with friends than on one's own. Especially when you don't know many people."

She had heard that everyone attended the Australia Day breakfast and award ceremony in the morning, with the town split between an afternoon at the Bowling Club and a community picnic at the Falls – Oxley Crossing's answer to Bondi, according to Marge Morris.

"Goodo then."

Since his intention had been to invite Sienna to go with him, her answer left Joey feeling more than a little crestfallen, but not for long. There was always another day.

"I'll see you there, then, Sienna. I've already put your name down to play on our team for the cricket match. Town versus country."

"But … Joey, I've never played cricket," Sienna couldn't hide her dismay.

"Nothing to it," she was assured. "Just pick up the bat and have a go. It's just for fun. Nothing serious."

"Well, okay. I guess, but doesn't anyone else have a say? I don't want to let you down, Joey."

"Nah," he discounted her fears. "Everyone joins in. You'll see."

He stayed chatting a few minutes longer, then rose to his feet.

"Better make a move before I get too comfortable. There's a pile of study waiting for me at home."

"Study?"

"Yeah. I decided it's time to make some changes in my life, so I signed up to an on-line training course. The notes for first semester arrived yesterday." Joey basked in the genuine interest he saw in Sienna's approving smile.

"I applied for one of the jobs Forestry is advertising locally as well. Hopefully the course will give me an edge. Decided I'd rather manage trees than simply chop them all down."

"Joey, I think that's wonderful. I wish you well with both moves."

"Thanks, Sienna. I'm going to stick with the study, whatever. As for the job, they ought to be making an announcement week after next."

"Fingers crossed!"

Looking back as he went through the gate, Joey saw a smiling Sienna holding up both hands with fingers crossed.

"Me too, Joey. Fingers crossed!" Gwynna called out, copying her mother's gesture.

"With all that luck coming my way, how can I lose? Bye girls." His own crossed fingers held high, Joey jogged across the street, disappearing from sight down the driveway of number 29.

THE MAKING OF JOEY LAMBERT

5

On Sunday morning Sienna unfolded her picnic chairs in a shady spot at the back of the crowd in Oxley Park. Taking her daughter by the hand, she went to buy breakfast for herself and Gwynna from the Lions Club barbecue, exchanging greetings with those around her, pleasantly surprised by how many of them she already knew. Although she did miss Josie Tan who'd had to return to her student job in Sydney.

Gary and Joy Smith, Sienna's parents, had never been deeply involved in their local community, so she was very new to country-style Australia Day festivities. Her ready acceptance into this community, filled her soul with a happy glow, making her mind up for her. She would be different. *She* would make a niche for herself and she would *belong*. She was done with being an outsider. The weird girl who lived at home with her parents and never went anywhere. Oxley Crossing was her home now and she was going to fit in.

Arriving at the head of the queue, she was giving her order to her neighbour, Lions member Mike Patterson, when Gwynna tugged on her shirt.

"Mum! Here's Clarry and Stell. Can they have breakfast with us? Please?"

Why not.

The Murphy twins had enjoyed plenty of her biscuits, fruit and sandwiches while playing with Gwynna during the last week. Sienna sometimes felt she had three daughters now instead of one. Make that four, she amended, catching sight of Molly waving and running up to them, a half-eaten bacon and egg burger clutched in her hand.

"Hungry, girls?" Even though it was obviously unnecessary, she included Molly in her question as well as Clarice and Estelle who hung their heads, bare toes stirring the dust.

"Tell Mr Patterson what you'd like," Sienna invited, not waiting for an answer. With grateful smiles, they did just that.

"Mr Patterson?" Estelle caught Mike as he was about to place their order with the cooks. "Mr Patterson, please, could you cut mine and Clarry's up so we can share with the others?"

The others? Sienna had almost forgotten the twins were the youngest of five children. Looking over her shoulder, she spotted the three older ones sitting on the grass under the trees. Looking as she had usually felt before The Crossing - like outsiders. Hungry outsiders. Her blood boiled. She hadn't met the parents yet, and hoped she never had to.

"Mike," she said impulsively, "instead of splitting, add three more burgers and orange juices to my order. Estelle, run and tell your brothers and sister to come and join us."

"No need to pay for the Murphys," Mike muttered when she handed over her payment.

"There's always something left over. We'd have given those kids a few pick-up jobs and paid with food. They wouldn't have starved. Not that sort of town."

"I know, Mike, but take it anyway. The Lions are raising money for charity. Consider it a donation."

"Good lass."

I try to be, Sienna thought as she herded the children back to where she'd left her chairs. *I try, and I'm going to try harder in future.*

"Ms Smith?"

Sienna looked up at Michael, the oldest of the Murphy siblings. He shuffled his feet, but held her gaze, even though his cheeks took on a tinge of red. Embarrassment made his voice gruff, reawakening her anger with his parents. This boy oughtn't to be made to feel shame for something so much not his fault.

"Ms Smith, thanks for buying breakfast for all of us. It's very kind of you. And thanks for letting the twins play with Gwynna. If there's ever anything I can do for you, let me know."

"Maybe there is, at that, Michael."

When she'd discussed the plight of these kids with Eddie Patterson, Eddie had stressed she needed to be careful to leave them with their pride. Not simply to throw her charity in their faces. She looked the boy over thoughtfully. At thirteen he was already taller than she was. Probably stronger, too.

Michael visibly braced himself.

"Mickey, Ms Smith. No-one calls me Michael."

"How are you at pushing a lawnmower, Mickey?" Sienna noted the relief flooding his features. "It's just that I really hate mowing. If you'd be willing to help out, I'll pay the going rate."

"First one's for free, Ms Smith. To show you how good a job I can do."

And to pay for breakfast this morning? Sienna rather suspected it was. Which just went to show the boy had integrity. And pride.

"Deal."

Sienna held out her hand, and, smiling shyly, the boy shook it.

"Deal," he repeated.

At that moment the roar of a small convoy of trucks had all heads turning. Cheers and whistles welcomed the arrival, in force, of the volunteer men and women serving on the town's Rural Fire Service and State Emergency Service who proudly waved miniature Aussie flags from the backs of gleaming trucks adorned with patriotic bunting.

"Look, Mum! There's Joey!"

But Sienna didn't need Gwynna's announcement. Her eyes had picked out his lanky form the instant the SES truck turned into the park; realising at the same moment she'd been unconsciously searching for him since the moment she'd arrived. Standing, along with everyone else, she cheered and waved her flag, eagerly meeting his eyes as he scanned the area. They lit up when he spotted her, and he waved back.

He was looking for me!

Sienna's heart did a short quickstep.

Trucks parked in a neat array flanking the low-loader designated to do duty as a temporary stage, the uniformed volunteers trooped over to the barbecue to grab their meals before the official proceedings began.

Burger and coffee in hand, Joey arrived beside Sienna's chair just as Elizabeth Tan, rounding up Gwynna's playmates who were wanted for choir duty, was leaving. Her warm greeting, accompanied as it was by a speculative glance from Joey to Sienna sent the blood rushing to both their cheeks. She laughed and winked, then trotted after the girls. Very carefully, Sienna avoided looking at Joey until the moment was safely in the past.

"I'm going to sit up front where I can see Molly and the twins when they sing. Wish I was in the choir, too."

"Next time, Gwyn," Sienna promised, waving Joey to the vacant chair at her side.

"You're looking very fine," she said, her admiring him in his crisp overalls and shiny helmet. Somehow, his short, luxuriant beard looked just right with the uniform. She'd noticed quite a few beards, of all varieties, among the younger men. Joey's looked so soft she half lifted a hand as if to stroke, but quickly lowered it to her lap. She didn't do touching. No way. Too personal. Her mind desperately searching for distraction from temptation, she remembered a poem she'd learnt in primary school. Apparently, as in Banjo Paterson's Iron Bark, beards were the 'in' fashion in Oxley Crossing. Lips twitching with a swallowed giggle, she turned a beaming smile on her companion.

"Can you stay, Joey, or do you have to rush off too?"

Joey stayed, singing lustily along when the school choir led off the program with the National Anthem.

Everyone else sang too, so Sienna lifted her own voice. The combined volume of the large crowd inspired a family of magpies to carol in counterpoint harmony from the gum trees bordering the park.

During the speeches and presentations which followed, Joey's irreverent thumbnail sketches of the civic dignitaries had Sienna giggling more than once. When Doctor Roberts, whom she had not yet been introduced to, was called up to receive a special award for his thirty-five years of service to the people of Oxley Crossing, she cheered just as loudly as those who knew him well.

These people, Sienna realised, were her friends and neighbours. The children singing in the choir and playing in the small brass band were students at her school. Snowy-haired Bill Whitman who gave the hecklers as good as he got, her Shire President, and his son Robert who presented the many annual awards, her elected representative in Canberra. This was *her* community.

Glowing with pleasure, Sienna felt as if she, too, had been awarded a prize.

The prize of a normal life.

The uncomfortable inner voice reminding her she wasn't altogether a normal girl, and never would be, was quickly supressed, before it could dampen her happy mood. Today she felt normal.

"And now I think we're about ready for the event you've all been waiting so patiently for," Bill Whitman boomed over the loudspeaker.

"The annual SES versus RFS tug-o-war. Lions Club volunteers will be coming round with buckets for your donations, so dig deep. They're all volunteers, people, and they rely on your generosity to continue protecting The Crossing. Now, enough said, let's head over to see if the RFS team can take out the Griff Morgan Trophy for the sixth year in a row."

"What's the Griff Morgan Trophy, Joey?"

Joey, steering Sienna through the crowd to a front row vantage point, answered in a rush.

"It's named for old Griff Morgan, our captain, Alan Morgan's Grandpa, who started the local volunteer fire brigade. When the SES came, someone thought up the idea of the tug-o-war to raise funds. Gotta go, Sienna. I'm on the SES team. Cheer for us, will you? We need all the help we can get."

While the teams prepared for battle, yellow-shirted Lions Club members with their buckets canvassed the crowd. Watching, Sienna was gob-smacked to see how quickly they were filling up, with high denomination notes as well as coins.

A small hand slipped into hers, and she looked down to see Gwynna had returned to her side.

"What are they doing, Mum?"

Sienna explained.

"There's Mickey Murphy. He's helping collect money too. Can I put some in his bucket, Mum?"

"Course you can."

Sienna pulled her wallet from her shoulder bag.

The handful of coins for Gwynna, and the small sheaf of notes for herself which she counted out left her cash strapped till payday, but there was always the plastic if she needed something urgently.

"Over here, Mickey," she called.

Obligingly he swerved in their direction to collect their offerings. As the collectors with their buckets left the field, Sienna heard more than one bet being laid on who the victors would be.

"The fire brigade appear to be favourites," Sienna commented to Eddie Patterson who'd come to stand on her other side. "Why is that?" She felt a wee bit indignant on Joey's behalf, to hear his SES team being slighted.

Eddie laughed.

"Wait till you see them," she advised. "They have a not-so-secret weapon in their dispatcher, Wal Piper from out on *Piper's Lane*. That's a property up the top end of the valley."

Just then Bart Gibson and Alan Morgan, RFS and SES captains respectively, led the two teams of eight strong, fit men marching onto the field from opposing sides. Playing up to the crowd, they took their places behind the white markers at either end of the heavy rope laid ready, a red handkerchief tied in the exact middle to coincide with a red line painted on the grass.

Police sergeant Don Matthews, referee for the match, stepped forward when they signalled their readiness. The teams took the strain. Don waited, hand raised, till there was dead silence, then he blew the whistle and it was on. For long, deafening minutes the crowd cheered their encouragement.

The marker crossed tantalisingly back and forth over the line, neither team conceding more than scant inches at any time. Gradually the men began to tire.

That was the moment anchor-man Wal Piper came into his own. Built like a draught horse, a very large draught horse, he began inching backwards, his team reeling the rope in as he went. The SES team fought to the last, but without an anchor to match Wal's impressive weight, they were outclassed. With a final triumphant heave from the victors, they were sent sprawling ignominiously across the line. The crowd erupted into a babble of cheers and catcalls as they picked themselves up, dusting themselves down before lining up for the presentation of the trophy.

After that, there was nothing to do other than pack up and go home. Sienna and Gwynna made sure the area they'd occupied was left clean and folded their chairs. Ready to cross Bridge Street on the short stroll back to Nymboida Street, Joey appeared at their side once more.

"I'm sorry you didn't win, Joey, but what a fun way to end the morning. And did you see how much money was raised! It was absolutely amazing."

"Pretty good, alright. We get equal shares, whoever wins, and Alan and Bart have been making their shopping lists, but this year we're giving some to those crews who lost their gear in the bushfires over on the coast. We all help one another in any way we can."

"I know. We'll see you out at Rainbow Falls."

"Don't forget you're on my team for cricket.

Not the most reassuring thought to take with her, Sienna mused, waving goodbye and taking Gwynna's hand. She'd probably be bowled out for a duck.

48

6

Rooster-tails of red dust hung in the air behind the stream of vehicles on the gravelled Rainbow Falls Road, with yet another trailing Sienna's car as she followed Geoff and Elizabeth Tan. She and Gwynna had explored widely during their first week in The Crossing, but they hadn't come here. Although the photos in the brochure Marge Morris had given her showed it to be a temptingly pretty spot, Sienna had been too aware of the lonely road through the bush to a destination far from friendly habitation. Not for her, she'd decided, even though Marge had called it The Crossing's answer to Bondi and the January heat wave made her long to immerse herself in cool water.

Today, surrounded by friends, she looked forward to finally seeing Rainbow Falls for herself. It didn't disappoint. Hidden from view until she rounded the last bend in the road, Morgan's Creek spurted out from the lip of the basalt escarpment, thundering into the deep plunge pool below. Gradually shallowing to a laughing cascade through tumbled boulders, the swimming hole stretched for almost two hundred metres, bounded by a wide expanse of freshly mown grass.

Back in the shade of the trees numerous family groups had staked their claims and settled in, leaving a broad circle of empty grass surrounding a freshly marked concrete cricket pitch in the middle.

Hefting her folding chairs and insulated cooler bag, Sienna followed the Tans to a spot roughly half-way along, where Eddie and Mike sat with a group of younger people.

"Righto, Bailey!" Jamie Wright, best mate of Molly's brother Bailey, sprang to his feet. "Let's hit the water! Last one in's It."

The boys, wildly tossing shirts in the general direction of their mothers, ran off. Molly, close on their heels, paused to look back.

"C'mon, Gwynna, or you'll be It!" she shouted.

"Mum, can I …?"

"Course you can, Darling. I'll be right along."

Sienna dumped her gear in a heap as Gwynna threw aside the dress she'd been wearing over her swimmers and galloped off after the others.

"Sit over here with us, Sienna," Elizabeth called, shuffling her chair to widen the circle.

"But, shouldn't I keep an eye on the kids?"

"No need, girl. Today is mothers' time off. See, there are lots of dads playing lifeguard. You sit down and get to know your neighbours."

Sure enough, a dozen or so men, drinks in hand, stood chatting at intervals along the creek bank, so Sienna obeyed, although not without her nerves jangling anxiously.

Her eyes strayed frequently to the water, which was crowded with children of all ages, from teens diving from a rocky ledge into the deepest hole next to the falls to toddlers splashing about in the shallows.

"You know Eddie and Mike and their daughter Megan and her husband, Jon and their little Chloe," Elizabeth said, introducing Sienna around the circle. "This is Geni and Ben and their baby, Luke," she came to the only couple in the circle Sienna had not previously met, adding, "Ben is your boss. He's principal of the school."

Conversation became general, with Sienna shyly doing more listening than talking. Shortly after the men unobtrusively made their way down to the bank, taking their turn to watch over the frolicking youngsters until a siren sounded.

"Better get the food out," Megan laughed. "Kids and lifeguards will be descending like a swarm of starving locusts any minute."

Thoroughly enjoying herself, Sienna voted the bush picnic even more enjoyable than the morning's events, and it only got better. People migrated from group to group, catching up with old friends. Quite a few wanting to take a look at the new teacher, especially those whose children might be in her class.

Or the young men attracted by her pretty face and curvy, petite figure. These latter caused the butterflies to stir nervously, but no-one overstepped the mark, and Sienna relaxed again. When Joey appeared, crouching down beside her chair, she greeted him with her rare, high-wattage smile.

The one reserved for people she truly liked and felt completely comfortable with.

He chatted amicably for a few minutes, then announced,

"Stealing Sienna, folks. Mum wants a chat, and says she's too settled to move an inch." He took Sienna by the hand, pulling her up from her chair. "C'mon, Sienna. You see that redhead with plaits chasing after Gwynna?"

He pointed to where the children were playing some complicated game of tag, and Sienna used the need to shade her eyes to retrieve her hand from his loose grip.

"She's my baby sister, Naomi. Mum likes to know the parents of kids her brood are friends with."

That's okay, then. Sienna relaxed again and strolled happily along at his side. For one horrified moment she'd thought his Mum wanted to vet her because she was Joey's friend.

~~~~~

"Here Lass. Sit down by me." Marti Lambert patted the blanket beside her. "Run along now, Son, and organise that game of cricket you've been looking forward to. You've brought Ms Smith to me and we're going to get to know one another, aren't we, Girl?"

"I hope so, Mrs Lambert. I like to know who my daughter's friends are. By the way, please call me Sienna. No need to be formal, is there?"

"No need whatsoever, Sienna dear," Mrs Lambert chuckled, the deep voice which belied her spare frame, warm and welcoming. On first impression, she rather thought she liked this young lady of Joey's. "I'm Marti to my friends, and I'm another one who likes to know what my tribe are up to. And who it is they're getting up to mischief with."
~~~~~

The two women smiled at each other, although Sienna was a little perplexed. Marti Lambert, friendly as she seemed, gave the impression of having an unstated agenda. Unless she was mistaken, Joey's mother saw a great deal more than she let on.

A bit like Eddie, Sienna thought, finding the observation reassuring.

"Mischief?" Sienna giggled, turning her head for a quick check-up on Gwynna and her mates. "That's a bit severe, don't you think? They're a well-behaved group of little girls, surely?"

"And will continue to be as long as we keep them close to our hearts while giving them freedom to grow. I've tried to do that with all of mine, and it must be working. The older ones are always happy to come home to the farm."

Sienna nodded. Marti had expressed her own parenting philosophy exactly. Giving Gwyneth that freedom to grow, to be normal, was what had motivated her to finally leave home. A move most might consider long overdue.

Marti paused a moment before adding, "Don't know what I would have done without Joey while my John was laid up. He's a good boy, Joey. Got his head screwed on straight and his heart in the right place, despite what *some* people say." A sniff signalled her disdain at what other, less perspicacious, people thought. "What do you think about this study scheme of his, Sienna?"

"I think any time someone sets out to improve their circumstances they ought to be encouraged. Don't you, Marti?"

"I do indeed." Marti chuckled again. She was enjoying herself hugely getting to know Joey's little girl.

The two of them continued to chat amicably, and it wasn't until much later Sienna realised how much information the older woman had painlessly extracted from her. Not any of her real secrets, but Marti Lambert now knew more about Sienna and Gwyneth Smith than anyone else in The Crossing. Strangely enough, she didn't feel a single word of it would be passed on.

"Mum. Sorry to steal Sienna away from you, but our side is fielding first, and we need her. Coming Sienna?"

Joey held his hand out to her. Sienna hesitated a moment before slowly taking it in her own to let him draw her to her feet. She could have got up unaided, but was afraid it would look odd if spurned such a simple gesture of assistance. Especially in front of Marti Lambert's shrewd eyes which missed nothing.

"Marti?" Sienna took a moment to say goodbye. "I've enjoyed meeting you. If Naomi wants to come to my house to play, that's fine by me."

"Likewise, Sienna dear."

~~~~~

"Doing a spot of matchmaking, Marti?"

Marti chuckled as her friend sat down in the spot Sienna had vacated.

"Afraid I'm encroaching on your turf, Eddie?" Marti snickered.

"No need. I was just getting acquainted with the girl. Her daughter appears to be Naomi's newest playmate, and you know how I like to meet the whole family when my kids team up with anyone new."
~~~~~

"That's true. She's a good girl. A bit on the young side to have a child Gwynna's age, though. There's some story she's not telling."

"Doesn't matter to me. Ed. I've got no right to start pot-calling. Not with *my* story." She laughed outright. "You're not into pot-calling either, for which I've always been very grateful. You've been a good friend to me and mine, Eddie. If anything comes of it, I think she just might do for our Joey."

"I agree. She could be the making of him, Marti."

But that was too much for Marti's maternal pride.

"He's doing very well making something of himself without any outside help. Although, love is a great motivator," she added, seeing she'd almost offended her friend.

~~~~~

After all her fears about being a team liability, thereby disappointing Joey, Sienna enjoyed herself tremendously. Not that she'd been a standout player by any means, but she'd diligently run down the balls which came whizzing past her, and when it was her turn to bat, she hadn't got out for a duck. Being run out for a score of three wasn't much better, but it had been her partner who'd made a poor judgement call.

She'd had a lot of laughs, made some new friends in her own age group, and gone home feeling she'd acquitted herself well. If anybody had noticed she was different, it hadn't mattered. Added to all that, she'd learnt something new about herself.

She'd been sitting on the sidelines, padded up ready to go out to bat when one of the older men had strolled up from the creek to watch the cricket.
~~~~~

He'd smiled, and, settling down in the empty chair at her side which Joey had been occupying till his turn at bat, introduced himself.

"John Lambert," he said, shaking her hand. "And you're Sienna Smith, the mother of that girl Gwynna my Naomi has latched onto." He nodded to where about a dozen or so girls were sitting together sipping cold drinks.

"Pleased to meet you, Mr Lambert."

So this is Joey's Dad. Sienna studied him surreptitiously from beneath lowered lashes, pleased with what she saw.

"It's so nice to see Gwynna making friends before school starts. She was a bit nervous about being the new girl in a place where everyone else would have known each other for years."

"No fear of that now," he chuckled. "Well done!" he shouted, his attention being caught by Joey scoring a boundary. "You're up next, aren't you? Nervous? Joey mentioned you've never played before."

"A bit. That ball's *hard*. And they bowl so *fast*. I'll probably get out for a duck, first ball, and our team is already trailing."

"It can be a bit daunting. Here's what I tell my kids. Keep your eye on the ball, and find the still place deep inside yourself where your power lives, then channel your inner Jedi."

He grinned self-consciously, nodding when Sienna gaped at him.

"Works every time," he assured her.

Right then Joey got a bit too carried away and skied a ball straight into the steady pair of hands at long off.

Amid the concerted groan, John Lambert helped Sienna to her feet.

"You're on, Sienna. Remember," he winked. "Inner Jedi."

And it worked, just like he said it would.

Sienna knew all about that still inner place he'd told her about. After all, she'd had years of practice in finding it since it was exactly the same place Dr Michaelson had taught her to access when she had her panic attacks. Only she'd never thought about applying it to other situations. Like cricket. It hadn't made her an instant Bradman, but she'd managed to deflect each of the balls she'd faced in her one and a half nerve-racking overs in the crease.

Three days later she was congratulating herself again at the end of her first full day in charge of her own class. They were a delightful bunch of children, ranging from good as gold to those with more than a hint of mischief in them. They'd keep her on her toes, but she felt confident she'd manage them okay, and if she had problems Mrs Marsden had her back.

I did it, she exulted. *Dr Michaelson told me to find the courage to claim back my life, and I have, for Gwynna's sake. One step at a time, just as she said, with this giant leap to full independence to finish.*

With friends and work added to the family support she'd grown up with, her life was full, productive, and, most importantly, happy. From the outside it looked completely normal.

Of course, there was still that last barrier.

The one she had accepted would always be a step too far.

A step she'd never be able to take, in spite of Dr Michaelson's assertion that all things were possible if the right motivation was present. An essential element of her womanhood had been damaged. Irreparably, Sienna believed, but she could live with being less than normal. She had to, for Gwynna's sake. She'd drawn a line, and as long as she kept everyone else on the other side of it, she'd be safe.

Until she wasn't.

Until her friend crossed the line.

7

Whistling to himself, Joey followed the sound of voices round to the back of Sienna's house where he found her watering her collection of pot-plants on her shady back patio. Gwyneth was regaling her with the important events of her own day.

"Afternoon, ladies. How was school? Here, flowers to mark such an auspicious occasion."

The question, as the greeting, was directed impartially at both Gwynna and Sienna, as were the two bunches of cellophane wrapped flowers he handed to them as they walked over to him.

Excited, Gwynna squealed and threw her arms around Joey's neck. A man giving her flowers made her feel all grown up.

A man giving her flowers made Sienna distinctly uncomfortable. It took an effort to smile and murmur her thanks.

"I'll just put them in water," she said, wanting a moment to herself. "While I'm there, I'll make coffee. You'll have one with me, won't you Joey?"

Naturally he accepted.

About to follow Sienna inside, he was foiled when she directed Gwynna to entertain their guest till she returned.

They chatted over the coffee, Gwynna drifting away to play in her room soon after she'd finished sharing her own news. It didn't take Joey long to work the conversation round to his goal in visiting, bearing flowers.

"There's a dance on in the town hall, Saturday night," he began. "The CWA ladies organise one every month to raise money for charity. Alcohol free," – he'd heard Sienna tell Geni she didn't drink when she'd been offered a glass of wine from the bottle Geni was sharing with Megan – "supper and cold drinks available. Kids are welcome, too," he added, thinking Sienna might not be able to line up a babysitter at short notice. On dance nights the older teenagers who usually fulfilled that role were generally booked out.

He took another sip from his mug. Striving to sound casual, he popped the question.

"I was thinking you might like to go with me, Sienna."

Is Joey Lambert asking me on a date?

That's what it sounded like, only she didn't do dates. Couldn't. Panic threatened.

"So, how about it?"

Joey put his mug down and reached across the table to take Sienna's hand. She blanched, snatching it back out of his grasp, her chair scraping on the timber deck. He reared back as if she'd slapped him.

"Sienna! What's wrong? All I did was ask you out on a date. You're acting as if I made some sort of dire threat."

She gasped, fighting back the panic. Fighting back tears. She should have seen this coming. Should have headed him off before he started having expectations she couldn't meet.

"I know. I know. Sorry Joey," she muttered, not meeting his eyes.

That was better. Reminding herself this was Joey, her friend, made it easier to regain control. Still, now she owed him some sort of explanation, though God only knew there was no plausible excuse for her over-the-top reaction. There wasn't one, short of the truth, and that was out of the question. Hadn't someone once said strength lay in not making excuses and explanations? To simply state the case and leave it at that?

Rattled though she was Sienna gave it her best shot, firming her voice and looking him squarely in the eye.

"I don't date, Joey."

"What? Never?"

"Never."

"That's weird."

"Are you calling me weird, Joey Lambert? Are you saying I'm weird because I don't want to go out with you?"

Sienna was on her feet, leaning over the table towards him, anger replacing shame and fear. Empowering anger.

"No! I'm only saying it's weird for a pretty girl to say she never goes on dates."

Now Joey was also on his feet, almost nose-to-nose with her.

He might have said more, only he heard Eddie Patterson's screen door squeak as it opened. Recollecting himself, he straightened, stepping backwards towards the driveway.

"I'm going, but all the same, Sienna, just because you won't go with me doesn't mean you have to miss the dance. You can always go by yourself. It's for charity, remember. You'll probably know just about everyone there."

His angry, scathing tone seared her heart, but before she could think of an answer, Joey about turned and stalked off down the driveway to the gate. Hearing Eddie call out to Mike, Sienna snatched up the coffee mugs and dashed inside. She liked Eddie, but wasn't up to a neighbourly chat over the back fence. Not this afternoon.

~~~~~

Of course, she wasn't going to their blasted dance.

Since Joey's invitation on Wednesday the CWA dance seemed to be the number one topic on everyone's mind. The young, single teachers, and a few married ones as well, were all going. She'd run into Megan Armitage in the supermarket, and her parting words had been "See you Saturday night." When she'd made some excuse to Eddie, she'd been treated to a gentle lecture.

"You really ought to come along, Dear. You've fitted into our little community so well, and really, that's what dance night is all about. We're so far removed from everywhere we have to rely on each other in an emergency, and events like our dances and picnics help build community spirit."

Resolve weakening, she'd promised Eddie she'd think about it.
~~~~~

Only all she could think about was how she'd lost Joey Lambert's friendship and support. Until he was gone, Sienna hadn't realised how important a role he'd come to play in her life. She missed him. Even her mother had commented just last night that she sounded a bit down. References to the heat, and busy days at work had satisfied her mother, but Sienna knew they weren't the cause of her blue mood.

Maybe Joey would go on his own as he'd said she could. Maybe … Sienna rolled the idea which had come to her around in her mind. Maybe if she went to the dance, she could make it up with Joey. She'd been watching for him, toying with the idea of staging an 'accidental' meeting, and knew he was avoiding her. She didn't think he'd have asked any other girl. He'd told her himself that he wasn't much of a ladies' man.

The more she considered a reconciliation at the dance, the stronger the idea took hold in her mind.

It was Molly's grandmother, Carol Tan's, invitation for Gwynna to join Molly in a sleepover at her house, "… so you'll be free to go to the dance and not worry about her, Sienna.", which finally decided her.

Damn it all, I'll go! I've even got that new dress I bought for Mum and Dad's anniversary.

All day Saturday she could barely choke down a single bite for the butterflies lunging violently round and round in her stomach, but she stuck to her decision. She would go to the dance and look for an opportunity to apologise to Joey. She still wouldn't go on a date with him, but she'd try not to make a personal insult of her stance.

~~~~~
~~~~~

Ending the daily call to her mother, Sienna shook her head over Joy's reaction to the news she was going out. Dancing.

No Mum, I'm really not sure at all I'm not being carelessly foolish, thank you very much.

Sienna thought it, but no way could she ever say it. Her mother's cloying overprotectiveness was a direct result of what had happened. Neither of her parents, any more than herself, had emerged unscathed from that nightmare experience, although it had affected them in very different ways.

Her mother's extreme nervous caution had almost undermined her own resolve tonight, but it couldn't be helped. By the time she'd soothed her to the point she could say goodnight and hang up, she was running late.

From the end of her street she could hear the strains of a hit from the middle of the last century wafting on the still air. Eddie had told her there'd be a mix of old and new, but surely Bing Crosbie classics were a bit dated, even for The Crossing where people clung to old customs in a way city folk did not. One block was too close to get the car out, so Sienna hurried along the uneven footpath as quickly as was safe in four-inch heels.

"There you are, Dear. Hang onto your ticket. There's a lucky door prize drawn at the end of the night." Smiling nervously at Eddie and her friend Barbara Morgan who were on ticket duty, Sienna stared, wide-eyed, about her. At the couples milling around the room at the end of the first set. At the band up on stage at the far end. At the women congregating in chattering clusters on one side of the floor while the men did the same on the other.

"Hey! Sienna! Over here."

Mandy Brock, another young teacher, called out to her, and, thankfully, Sienna hurried to join her. Grateful not to be the odd one out a moment longer. The next dance was a modern, up-beat disco number and she let her friends draw her into their group dancing together to steps she easily got the hang of. A foxtrot followed. Ben Wright, her principal, led her out, his conversation an innocuous discussion on how well she'd been assimilated into both school and wider community. Geoff Tan claimed her in a rather lethargic attempt at keeping time with another fast song she'd heard on the radio quite often last year.

"Not much of a dancer," he apologised.

No kidding? Sienna grinned at him, enjoying herself anyway.

"Have to give it a whirl though, or my Lizzie gets cranky with me."

This time she laughed out loud. Somehow, she simply couldn't see Elizabeth Tan, an elegant livewire, as a Lizzie. Nerves forgotten, she quickstepped with Mike Patterson and jived with Peter Crawford, another teacher. She knew everybody, she realised. No strangers here to cause her concerns.

Then Joey Lambert stepped in front of her just as a waltz was called. Sienna's heartbeat accelerated. She'd looked for him. Not seeing him, she'd assumed he hadn't come. Now here he was.

"Dance this one with me, Sienna?"

Oh yes! Her hazel eyes glowed more green than brown.

"Of course, Joey." Sienna slid easily into his arms as the opening bars of the *Blue Danube* flowed through the hall. "I'm really glad to see you, you know." Sienna's nerves skittered, but she refused to give way.

"I owe you an apology. We're friends. I shouldn't have got cranky with you the other day, Joey. I'm sorry." Eyes darkening anxiously, she gazed up at him.

"No need to apologise to me, Sienna. You'd think by now I'd be used to pretty girls telling me 'no'. I guess it's because you're special, I couldn't laugh it off. Are we good again?"

Special. Joey thinks I'm special.

Heart sinking, Sienna fought back tears. The middle of a dance, her first dance ever, was not the place to turn on the waterworks. Joey's words ought to have made her happy, only she mustn't let him think like that. She mustn't let him expect more of her than she could give. How to get that across without losing the friendship she valued?

"All good. I like being friends with you Joey, but I'm nothing special. Please, don't ever think that I am."

Sienna didn't register the tremor in her lower lip, but Joey, a puzzled frown shadowing his brow, did. And had she emphasised the word 'friends' ever so slightly? He'd need to think about the hidden meaning he sensed lurking behind her words, but for that, he'd need a bit more quiet than he'd find here.

"Sure thing, Sienna. What did you think of …?"

For the rest of their waltz he kept the conversation light and inconsequential. Friendly. Impersonal. Until the music wound to a close.

"It's the supper interval, Sienna. Sit with me?"

"Sure, Joey, but first …" Sienna gestured towards the corridor at the back of the hall.

At Joey's understanding nod, she walked off quickly, too intent on reaching the ladies restroom to notice the people she was passing on the way.

"Joey."

"Oh, hi Sergeant."

Don Matthews hitched his belt, his eyes roving casually over the crowd. There was rarely any trouble at these dances, but he liked to put in an appearance, all the same. Sometimes the sight of a police uniform was enough to make some young idiot have second thoughts. Better thoughts.

"How's the study program going?"

Did everybody in town know? He hoped not. He could do without the added pressure that would put on him.

"Pretty good. My first assignment got a higher mark than I expected." At first glance he'd thought the 'D' on his paper meant he'd failed. When he realised it was a 'D' for 'Distinction' he'd whooped for joy.

"Reckon it made all the difference when I interviewed for that Forestry job yesterday." He'd meant Sienna to be the first person he told, but she'd been in a tricky mood, distracting him. Reminded by the sergeant's friendly enquiry, he couldn't hold it in a moment longer. "They called me this arvo to say I got it. I start in the nursery up the road next month."

"Well done, boy. I always knew you had it in you to be more than a yard hand at the saw-mill."

Don's congratulatory clap him on the shoulder, rocked Joey back on his heels. When he steadied, he was facing towards the back of the hall.

His first instinct was blazing fury. Sienna gave him the brush-off, but let some stranger from out of town maul her about in front of everybody!

Gripped in helpless thrall by deathly black fear of a full-blown panic attack, Sienna looked up. Desperately searching for a rescuer. Seeing none. Unable to do more than push feebly at the stranger who'd locked his arm around her shoulders, breathing choking beer fumes into her face, she caught Joey Lambert's eyes. A silent plea winged its way down the hall.

God, she looks like a roo caught in the headlights the moment before being skittled! Joey's eyes narrowed. That bloke was no friend of Sienna's. She was struggling to get free of him.

His fury returned, but this time it was levelled at a new target. His hands came out of his pockets where they'd been comfortably lodged. Came out as tightly clenched fists. Against the flow, he shouldered his way through the press of bodies making their way into the supper room.

Thank God! Sienna saw the exact moment Joey realised her plight and came rushing to her aid. Knowing she was no longer on her own added strength to her struggles.

"Let me go!" In her mind, Sienna yelled. In reality, it came out as a barely audible squeak. "Let me go!" This time her protest was accompanied by a four-inch heel plunged into the soft upper of a Nike tennis shoe.

"Aagh! Don't be like that, Love," her assailant slurred. "I can show a pretty little thing like you a much better time than these country yokels." He tightened his hold, his hand slipping forward to land on her breast, giving it a squeeze as he spoke.

"Take your filthy hands off her!"

Joey grabbed the bloke by the front of his shirt, loosening a couple of buttons as he yanked him away from Sienna. He raised his fist, ready to give the bastard what he deserved, when he was restrained by a strong hand gripping him implacably from behind.

"Steady on, Son," Sergeant Matthews said in Joey's ear. Voice far colder, and considerably louder, he addressed the bloke holding Sienna captive. "The lady said to let her go. I suggest you do just that. Now!" he added when compliance to his initial order was too slow. "You too, Lambert. Leave this to me."

Reluctantly, Joey opened his fingers and stepped back, staying at the sergeant's shoulder in case he got another chance to land a punch. His assistance wasn't needed. It was the work of seconds for Don Matthews to whip the miscreant's arm up behind his back and slap the cuffs on.

"You'll be coming with me, Mate. Drunk and disorderly for a start, I reckon. I can add assault, if you'd like to press charges, Ms Smith."

Sick to her stomach and growing sicker by the minute, Sienna mutely shook her head.

"Joey, fetch Eddie to take care of Sienna."

"No need, Sarge. Sienna's with me. I'll take care of her."

"Good lad. Then I'll be off to the station with this waste of space. I've got a nice, cosy cell waiting for him."

Sergeant Matthews frogmarched his prisoner off. Joey watching, frustrated anger still smouldering in his eyes.

Satisfied that Don was in full control of the situation, he turned back to offer comfort to Sienna. One thing he'd learnt for certain during the last ten minutes, Sienna Smith was very much 'his girl'.

"Here, Sienna, Love. Come and sit down out of the way till you feel a bit more up to scratch. The hide of that bastard, thinking he can come waltzing in here throwing his weight around."

He put his arm around Sienna's shoulders, unconsciously mimicking the other man's unwelcome embrace. Wrenching herself free from his much looser hold, Sienna cupped her hands over her mouth.

"I'm going to be sick," she moaned, running off to the ladies' restroom again.

Leaving Joey, open-mouthed, staring after her.

The sergeant's departure with his prisoner had stirred up the expected interest and speculation, but so far, few people were aware of what had really taken place at the back of the hall.

Angie Wilson who'd been on a similar errand to Sienna was one of them. Arriving on the scene mere seconds after Joey and Don, and mindful of being five months pregnant, she'd remained at a safe distance throughout, her shrewd brain processing the scene. She reckoned Sienna would be more appreciative of a woman's comfort than any man's; even if the man was her boyfriend. She wasn't sure she had that entirely correct, but judging by Joey's reaction earlier, she suspected they were more than just friends.

"I'll go to her, Joey," she murmured, patting him on the shoulder when she caught up to him outside the ladies'.

"You go fetch her a cup of tea. Make it strong and sweet. And one for me, too, while you're at it."

8

The anteroom furnished with a chaise longue and a comfortable armchair was empty. Following the sound of running water, Angie proceeded into the adjoining room where, as expected, she found Sienna Smith hanging over a basin. A clean basin. Either her stomach had failed to disgorge its contents, or she'd washed the evidence down the sink. Either way, Angie, not long past the throes of morning sickness, was profoundly grateful.

Tears tracked down the girl's blanched face. Tap water flowed unnoticed, a dreadful waste in the middle of the worst drought in living memory, even though Oxley Crossing wasn't as badly off as places further west. Reaching forward, Angie turned the tap off. Pulling a handful of paper towels from the dispenser, she gently thrust them into Sienna's hands.

"Dry your face, Sienna," she ordered, firmly, but not unkindly. "Are you going to be sick? If not, let's go sit down in the other room." Ushering the younger woman into the chair, she turned to lock the door.

"What if s...s...someone needs to come in?" Sienna hiccupped, burying her face in the wad of paper towels.

"Oh, Hell. You're right. These are the only women's toilets in the damned place." Angie unlocked the door again. "Turn that chair to face me," she instructed, lowering herself full-length onto the chaise. Wriggling to get comfortable, she elevated her baby-belly as prominently as possible. "There. If anyone does intrude, you're just keeping me company while I have a little rest. Leave the talking to me."

Goggle-eyed, Sienna had been following the pantomime.

"Why are you doing this?" she whispered.

"What? Helping you?"

Sienna nodded.

"We women ought to stand by one another, don't you think?" Sienna nodded again. "I haven't always been a farmer's wife," Angie said. "For quite a while I was a barmaid in a pretty rough part of Sydney. Got to see plenty of the seamier side. Just now, I saw some of what happened out there, and Sienna, you looked to me like a girl who had just been violently reminded of some pretty awful occurrence from her past. I'm right, aren't I?"

Unfocused eyes trained on the lapful of shredded pulp to which her trembling hands had reduced the paper towels, Sienna nodded mutely once more.

"I don't need to know the details, that's your business, but, Sienna, whatever happened to you, you're not the first girl it's happened to, and you won't be the last. Unfortunately. Now, blow your nose," she pushed the box of tissues on the table between them a little closer to Sienna. "Take a few deep breaths, and when you're ready, we'll work out what comes next. That's the important part."

To Sienna, used to her mother's coddling whenever she got upset, Angie's matter-of-fact common-sense attitude was bracing. She found herself obeying without protest. Outwardly, her hands stilled their obsessive shredding of paper, her tears dried, and except for the reddened eyes and blotchy cheeks left in their wake, she looked quite calm. Inside, she was still a quivering mass of nerves.

"I want to go home."

"As soon as you're ready."

"Only, …" a pitiful quivering of her lips almost betrayed her hard-won composure. "Only I … I'm scared. I'm too scared to walk home alone. In the dark."

"You'll be quite safe. Sergeant Matthews hauled that drunken idiot off to the cells to sober up."

Sienna seemed to shrivel before Angie's eyes, and for a moment, she thought the waterworks were about to start again. Sighing, she realised the girl was in no fit state to make her own way home.

"Shall I fetch Joey to walk with you?"

"No." Sienna was sure the alacrity of her refusal was an insult to Joey, but she couldn't help it. Sergeant Matthews, in his reassuring police uniform, was the only man she might have felt comfortable with right now, and he'd already left.

This time it was Angie who nodded slowly. Who, blessedly, seemed to understand.

"Alright, then. We'll slip out the back door, and I'll walk you home. Okay, Sienna?"

"O…okay."

And so they did. Angie waved off Joey, returning with the teas, quietly asking him to tell her husband, Alan, she'd be back soon, and they made their getaway through the fire-escape door, virtually unnoticed.

~~~~

Awake long before the kookaburras down by the creek cackled their joyous salute to the dawn, Joey Lambert paced restlessly, his eyes flicking to the clock every few seconds. Minutes felt as long as hours, and hours were eternities. Angie had assured him she had delivered Sienna safely to her home, where she'd eventually left her calm and, if still shaken, at least coping behind the locked doors of her own home.

"She'll be okay, Joey," Angie had said, giving him a sympathetic pat on his arm. "She packed up herself and her daughter and came out here, away from her home and family. That took guts, Joey. Sienna's stronger than she thinks. Last night she had a bit of a shock, but give her some space, and she'll bounce back in no time. You'll see."

He knew Sienna was strong, and Angie was undoubtedly right in saying she'd bounce back. What had Joey's guts tying themselves in knots was the thought of what had caused Sienna to fall apart when confronted by a dropkick any other girl would have dealt with without batting an eye. If what he suspected was true …

He wrapped his arms around himself, wishing they were wrapped around Sienna. He wanted to hold her, safe and secure in his arms forever.
~~~~

Protect her from harm.

Go back in time and rescue her from whatever had put the fearful shadows he'd noticed more than once, into her lovely greeny-brown eyes.

Impossible, of course, but he loved her, and wanted to keep her safe.

Joey stilled, his last thought replaying in his mind. He loved her. Loved Sienna Smith. But … were his protective instincts really love? Couldn't be. Could they? He wasn't feeling all loopy and romantic; what he thought he ought to feel if he was in love. The strongest emotion he'd been feeling for hours past, since last night, in fact, was anger. A red-hot rage at whoever had harmed Sienna. And anxiety. Gnawing anxiety - for Sienna. His thoughts slowed, reeled back to the moments preceding the incident which had precipitated everything he felt now, to holding Sienna in his arms while they waltzed. He'd felt pretty loopy and romantic then. Considering further, he realised that was the way she'd had him feeling since the first time they met.

"Bloody Hell," he murmured aloud. Sienna was at the heart of everything he'd done, everything he'd felt. "I am in love. Must be. Damn it all, I'm in love with Sienna."

That set him back on his heels. Love came with built-in consequences. Responsibilities. He sat down heavily on the edge of his bed, overwhelmed. Afraid. His chest constricted so tightly he couldn't breathe. He wasn't ready. He gasped, his heart pounding as if it was about to burst out of his chest. Just when he was sure he was dying the pressure eased. Miraculously, he could breathe again.

After a couple more heavy thuds, his heart resumed its usual rhythm. Almost. It was still running faster than was comfortable.

What the Hell happened to me?

Love, his inner self replied. *Love happened.*

Ready or not, he was in love. That sneaky little bugger, Cupid, had got him good and proper. Instinctively, Joey knew this was the real deal. Warmth, strengthening warmth, permeated his whole body.

"I am ready," he whispered, then louder, "I am ready."

He couldn't wait to … tell … Sienna. His racing thoughts skidded to an abrupt halt.

Sienna.

He couldn't tell Sienna.

She'd laugh at him.

The Good Lord knew, he was nobody's hero. Even his sisters, who loved him unconditionally, called him a galah. The whole damned town did. And they were right. He dropped his head into his hands.

"No, they flaming well aren't!" Joey thumped a fist on his thigh, then jumped to his feet, pacing back and forth as far as the confines of his small bedroom allowed.

It used to be true. He used to be a stupid bloody galah, but not any longer. He'd gotten his act together. Just look at the study he'd undertaken, that he was doing well at. The new job he'd start in a couple of weeks. The interviewer had told him that if he met their requirements, Forestry would put him through a botany degree.

Now he loved Sienna, he'd be even more motivated to make something of himself.

Sienna.

Joey threw himself back down on the bed.

Thinking.

It was on the day they met he'd taken the bull by the horns and signed up to improve himself and his prospects. She really was at the heart of his new life. A goofy smile spread across his rather ordinary face, and the whole world took on a rosier aspect.

Maybe she wouldn't laugh at him.

Sienna wasn't the sort to callously hurt a guy's feelings. Still, maybe he'd better hold off telling her how he felt. Until she could see for herself that he had something to offer a girl like her.

Then he remembered, and his heart plummeted. Sienna had problems of her own. Demons of her own.

Joey got up and made himself a mug of coffee. If he was going to help Sienna, slay dragons for her, he needed to think hard before he jumped in with his size twelve Blundstones making a difficult situation worse.

Love. Joey shook his head. Whoever would've thought. He straightened, feeling ... He pondered just what he was feeling, then realised; he felt more. More himself. More himself than he'd ever imagined himself to be.

Whatever it took to solve Sienna's problems, he was up for it; though he'd tread carefully.

~~~~~
~~~~~

Dressed in his best jeans, a neatly pressed charcoal, short-sleeved shirt, and freshly polished tan Blundstones - the good ones, not the battered old ones he wore to work - Joey opened the gate.

At the last minute he'd slipped the plaited kangaroo-skin belt his mother had given him for Christmas through the loops on his jeans. His mother liked Sienna. She'd told him so, and she didn't say things like that unless she meant them. As he dressed, he'd felt he was putting on armour. Preparing himself for battle, although, God knew, he was no Galahad.

Slowly, deliberately, he mounted the three steps leading to Sienna's navy-blue front door adorned with a gleaming brass lion's head knocker he'd never consciously noticed before.

He grimaced at the fanciful turn his thoughts had taken. He couldn't afford to let them stray as they had a tendency to do. Not this morning. A Lee Kernaghan hit from a couple of years back rose into the still morning air, and he turned his head. Raising a hand, he gave Eddie a wave. A good old stick, she hadn't asked a single question when he'd phoned, asking her to be out front, and there she was, minding her own business, sipping tea on her front veranda with the radio loud enough to ensure privacy for the conversation he was set on having with Sienna. Needed to have with her.

Feet planted at parade rest on the mat informing him friends were welcome, he breathed deeply, mentally girding his loins, then took the lion's head in his hand and rapped smartly. And waited.

About to knock again, he noticed movement behind the lead-light panel set into the upper half of the door.

Recognised the shadowy shape of Sienna. And braced himself. Last night she'd rejected his support. If she was still of that mind, all his careful preparations would go for nought.

"Joey! What are you doing here?"

He gave her a critical once-over. She looked a heap better than when he'd last seen her, sneaking out the fire-escape, leaning heavily on Angie's arm. Heaps better, despite the dark circles under eyes whose brilliance was dulled this morning to a drab brown. He liked it better when they glowed green with happiness. How would they look when they radiated love? He gulped, sternly ordering his mind back to the present.

"Morning, Sienna. I thought I'd just look in to see you're alright. After last night." Nervous fingers tugged at his collar as if it was constricting him, although that was physically impossible with an open-necked shirt.

"I am, Joey. Thank you."

She held the door open wider. Joey stepped back, off the mat, pleased when Sienna followed him onto the veranda, even though one hand still gripped the edge of the door.

"Can we talk?" He gestured towards the cane chairs a bit further along the veranda.

Sienna hesitated, then shrugged lightly, and nodded. Her behaviour last night had been far from normal, and, guessing Joey, among others, might have questions, she'd given some thought to her answers.

How much to reveal.

How much to conceal.

"Wait here while I fetch some coffee."

Suddenly her careful preparation counted for nothing. Hastily, she retreated to the kitchen to regroup. She took her time. A steely determination she'd never seen in Joey before told her he'd still be there, waiting, until he got what he came for. She warmed a plate of mini quiches in the microwave. Took the time to make strong, fragrant brewed coffee, instead of quick and easy instant. Set a tray with plates, cups and saucers and linen napkins the way her mother did for special visitors. Finally, with no fresh avenues for delay, she picked up her tray and headed out to the veranda.

To Joey.

9

"I haven't had breakfast, yet." Sienna poured coffee and offered the quiches to her guest before taking her place at the table.

"Neither have I."

After his momentous discoveries since waking, Joey wasn't surprised he'd forgotten to eat. He'd even let the coffee he'd made go cold, ending up tipping it down the sink. His stomach rumbled, so he tucked into the food. He'd almost finished the three portions he'd claimed for himself before he noticed Sienna had barely taken a nibble from her first.

"Not hungry?" He felt greedy, scoffing down his breakfast while she sat there toying with her food.

Greedy. And guilty. And a stupid bloody idiot.

Seduced by food, he'd let himself be diverted from his difficult purpose. Far from stupid, Sienna had to know he wanted to talk about last night, and here she was, so plagued by nerves she couldn't eat. With a regretful glance at the two mouthfuls remaining on his plate, Joey pushed it away from him.

"You're a great cook, Sienna, but I've had enough." Recalling something else he'd let slip from his mind, he cocked his head, listening for noise from inside. "Where's Gwynny? She still asleep?"

"Not home yet." Pleating her napkin, then smoothing it flat again, Sienna flashed an upward glance from beneath her lashes, reluctant to admit she was alone. "Elizabeth and Geoff are taking their kids for a swim at the falls, and a barbecue lunch. Gwyneth too."

"Good." That shocked a direct stare from her. Freed from the restraint imposed by a child's presence, Joey ploughed straight in. "I'm glad there are no kids hanging about, overhearing things they're too young to understand."

Sienna fell back to her nervous pleating, panic fluttering its wings at the edges of her consciousness. Joey wasn't sticking to the script she'd rehearsed in her mind.

Distracted by Sienna's nimble fingers, Joey reached out and gently removed the napkin from her grasp, tossing it down on top of his own. Her eyes tracked it, then snapped back to meet his full-on when he captured her hands, firmly holding them still on top of the table. She tugged, surprised when he refused to release her.

Joey hitched his chair closer to Sienna's side.

"Sienna."

Gasping, she tugged again. Trying to free her hands. Escape.

Now it was Joey about to fly into a panic. What the bloody Hell did he do now? He recalled how Sienna had responded to Angie's firm handling the night before.

"Stop that!" Pleased with the way the command, issued smoothly and calmly from his lips, stilled Sienna's struggle to escape, he gave her hands a little shake and continued.

"I'm your friend, Joey Lambert, remember? Just about the least scary bloke on the face of the Earth. I just want you to sit still and listen. You're not here alone with some bastard out to hurt you. This is Sunday morning in the middle of Oxley Crossing. Eddie Patterson is reading the Sunday papers over there," he carefully lifted one of his hands from hers to point.

"One screech, and she'd be here in a flash giving me a clip around the ears. If she's not enough, I can see Hazel Whitman dead heading her roses." He hadn't arranged for Hazel's presence, but he'd accept whatever gifts the gods sent. "If we took the trouble to look, there's probably a dozen more like them within earshot. Okay?"

Quiescent now, Sienna nodded. Joey released his remaining grip on her hands.

"You're free as a bird, Sienna. You can jump up and go scurrying back inside like a frightened little mouse. Any time you want. I won't stop you."

A frightened little mouse? I'm not! If I'm a bit nervous sometimes, it's because I've got reason to be. Really, I'm brave as a lion.

Sienna reminded herself of the courage she'd shown in so many aspects of her life, but Joey didn't know about all that. She'd have to prove her courage, if she wanted him to see who she truly was.

And that was definitely not a mouse.

It damn near broke Joey's heart, speaking so harshly, when all he wanted was to hold Sienna close and protect her from the world's slings and arrows. He took a couple of quick breaths, hardly able to believe his luck when she not only sat where she was, but gave him a trembling ghost of a smile.

"I lo... like you, Sienna. Care about you. I want to help you, and I believe I can." He wasn't as certain as he sounded, but he'd give it a bloody good try. If she'd let him. "Will you listen?"

Sienna nodded, then, feeling more was needed, squeezed out a strangled "Yes."

Joey might think he wasn't a bit scary, but just now he looked positively fierce. Fierce *for her*. A sense of relief washed over Sienna. Warmth began melting the ice encasing her heart. She'd thought she had to face her fears alone, now she'd left home, only she wasn't alone. Joey was here with her.

For her.

Moving to Oxley Crossing *had* been the right thing for her. The next step. The downside had been finding herself cut off from the support of her parents and Dr Michaelson. They were only a phone call away, but the distance meant her parents would worry themselves sick if they felt she wasn't coping. Which was why she made herself sound totally upbeat in their nightly chats. And she tried to stick to office hours with Dr Michaelson whom she knew had a family of her own, and other patients whose current situations were worse than hers.

Stealing a glance at Joey, she was hurt to see anxiety clouding his face.

Anxiety for her.

Greatly daring, she lifted her hand and slid it across the table, nudging his tightly curled fingers. When, startled, he automatically opened them, she placed her hand lightly within his. And smiled. Not her best smile by any means, but a brighter one than a moment before.

Grateful, Joey smiled back. Gently rubbing his thumb over Sienna's knuckles, he gathered his thoughts. Now came the hard part.

"I've got a cousin, Laura," he began. "She's my age, and we've always been best mates. She's a nurse. Used to work at Tamworth hospital. She used to share a flat with a girl she trained with. Last year, her friend's brother called round to see his sister. Or so he said. Laura told him Penny wasn't due home for an hour or so. He asked to wait, so she let him in. She'd met him a few times. Didn't particularly like him, but didn't see any harm in him."

"Joey! Joey, stop," Sienna interrupted, gripping his hand hard enough to make him wince. She could see where this story was going. "You shouldn't be telling me this. It's breaking trust with your cousin, don't you see?"

"No, it's okay, Sienna." If Joey hadn't already been in love with her, her concern for Laura would have tipped him over the edge. "I phoned her. Asked permission. I just told her I thought it might help a girl I knew. No names, Sienna. She said okay, and that if it was relevant, she'd be willing to talk to you if it would help you."

Sienna relaxed. "Go on, then."

"Yeah, well. You've obviously guessed what happened so I won't go into details. He knocked her around a bit. She's only a little thing like you, and there was no way she could fight him off." Joey hesitated a moment, then ploughed on.

"When he finished, he threatened to come back and do her in if she said a word to anyone. Well, there may not be much to our Laura, but she's no coward. As soon as he was out the door, she called the police."

Sienna, wide-eyed and pale, gave his hand a sympathetic squeeze.

"It went to court, but it was a he said, she said case and his lawyer's a slimy bastard who twisted the facts to make Laura look bad. Got him off, but he's known to the police now. They're watching him, and if he tries it with again with some other girl, hopefully they'll make it stick."

"How's Laura now?" Sienna's voice shook. She shook all over, placing herself in Laura's shoes. Not at all hard for her to do. They felt so much like her own.

"She's getting better. She couldn't stay in Tamworth. She copped a heap of abuse from the bloke's family and was scared to set foot outside. Moved to Brisbane where she lives with one of Mum's sisters. Last month she started work at a women's health clinic. No male staff. Reckons she can't face working with men just yet, but she's determined not to let being raped define her life. Who she is."

There. He'd uttered the 'r' word. He'd been skating round it for the last ten minutes, but now it was out there. Joey could almost see the letters shimmering red and portentous in the air between them.

"She absolutely right, Joey."

Her chest was so tight she felt her heart might burst, but Sienna held on.

Laura had offered to help *her*, but Laura's pain was fresher than hers. Maybe *she* could help Laura. She'd had years of counselling from one of the best. "Is she receiving help, Joey? Counselling?"

"Yeah, she is. Says it's making a difference. Where she works now, some of their clients are in similar situations, and she says that helps too. Knowing she's not the only one."

It would. I never had that, but I think it would have helped.

"Sienna," Joey sounded really nervous, his hand clutching hers tighter than she felt comfortable with, but after one look at his face, Sienna let him.

"Sienna, you know what I think, don't you? Why I told you about Laura? There're so many odd little things about you that seemed familiar, and last night, your reaction was just like Laura's when a bloke came up to her in a pub where we'd gone for dinner. It just clicked in my mind. You've been raped too, haven't you? And you're still finding your way?"

Sienna sat absolutely still. Frozen. Eyes fixed on a spot a million miles away. She was lost in her own mind for so long Joey thought she wasn't going to answer him. Thought he'd blown it. Even her hand, still lying in his clasp, felt icy.

He didn't know what to do! He was near panic when she gave a little shudder and turned to look straight at him, her eyes still focused far away.

"Yes."

"Oh, God, Sienna. I'm so sorry. So sorry. I never should have brought it up. Should have let sleeping dogs lie."

"Only it wasn't you who woke them, Joey. That happened last night, when that bloke grabbed me and breathed beer fumes all over me." Sienna was seeing him now, curiosity edging out remembered horror. "Why did you bring all this up?"

"I thought I could help. Maybe. Wanted to. Only now … Maybe it's above my pay grade and I've only made it worse for you. I'm sorry, Sienna. I really am."

Eyes narrowed, Sienna studied him, as if trying to see into his soul. He felt she wasn't much liking what she saw there, and squirmed in his chair. Releasing her, he dropped his hands into his lap, lowering his head so he could no longer see the expression on her face.

Sighing, she shifted on her chair. Joey lifted his head, watching her warily.

"Your intentions were good. What sort of help did you imagine you might offer?"

He couldn't believe it. Was she taking him seriously?

"Oh, you know. Be there for you. Be a buffer between you and people who make you nervous. Be someone you could talk to. You know." Joey trailed to a stop, hunching his shoulders against an imagined blow. Even to himself he sounded vague. Ineffectual. Totally bloody useless. He couldn't find the words to express what lay in his heart. Annoyed with his failure he burst out, "Damn it all, Sienna. We're friends. I care."

Unbelievably, she smiled. The radiant smile that made him feel good.

Special.

Not a stupid drongo.

"A friend is exactly what I need most. A friend who cares enough to stand up and be counted when the chips are down. You are that kind of friend, aren't you, Joey Lambert? This wasn't easy for you, was it?"

She'd been afraid he felt more for her than she could accept. Afraid his chivalrous nature would lead him to mistake their easy friendship for something she'd never be able to feel for any man. She'd dreaded hearing him blather on about being in love with her. But he hadn't. He'd offered her precisely what she needed most. A friend.

"Hardest bloody thing I've ever done."

"As well as panic attacks like last night, I get black moods. Fits of depression. Reckon you could cope with that?"

"I'll give it a bloody good try."

"Then I reckon we've got a deal, Joey Lambert. I accept you as my friend. Not that I didn't already count you as one."

This time she didn't just smile. The grin she gave Joey was priceless.

He grinned back, but his was shadowed by the fear he'd fail her when she needed him the most.

10

Relieved as she was Joey wasn't asking difficult questions, Sienna knew she couldn't leave it like that. She'd read the shadows behind his lop-sided grin.

He deserved the truth.

How else would he know how to defeat the demons she faced when the debilitating blackness closed in over her head? It didn't happen often, thank goodness, or she'd never have been able to take up a teaching career. Never have been able to function almost normally. Never have been able to leave the house. She'd been there, and would rather die than go back to that pitiful existence. That wasn't any kind of a life.

It wasn't even as if her story was some deep, dark secret. How could it be, when it had been blazoned all over the television news, the radio and newspapers of the day? Of course, there was more to it than had ever been reported, although a clever hacker, or someone with access to the police files might be able to piece it together.

As a gesture of trust, she owed Joey the truth.

The only question was, how much of the truth? She wouldn't be the only one to suffer if some distorted version leaked out. She couldn't bear it if her baby, Gwyneth, was smeared. The way people lived on social media there was always the possibility of a leak, but she trusted Joey not to do that to her.

Damn it all, Sienna, stop dithering. After Laura, he'll understand. Just tell the man.

"Joey, if you're going to be my champion, like you say, you ought to know where I'm at. Are you up for it?"

She'd sounded steady. Casual almost. Inside, Sienna was a mass of quivering nerve-ends. She'd talked about *everything* with Dr Michaelson. *Everything.* But she'd never spoken to anyone else, not even her Mum, about the worst of it. Now she felt the need to share her story with Joey. It was selfish of her, but it would almost be a relief to share it. If he knew, he'd be someone she could talk to when the black moods hit. He could help her talk her way through them.

"Up for it? Sienna, if you can bear to tell, the least I can do is listen. Course I'm up for it." He was almost insulted she'd felt the need to ask.

"Okay then. It's a bit different to what happened to your cousin, Laura. They were strangers. They grabbed me off the street when I was on my way home from a piano lesson. On Easter Thursday. I ..."

"Wait! Wait a moment. They? How many Sienna?"

She stared at him, her heart contracting painfully.

She'd hardly begun, and already he was consumed by rage. Disgust? Maybe this wasn't such a good idea after all.

Only … She'd started, and he was waiting for her answer. She clenched her hands in her lap. So tightly the bones crackled.

"Three. Three men in their twenties."

"How old were you?"

Sienna edged back a little from where Joey's white-knuckled fists lay ready for action on the table.

"Thir…Thirteen. Almost fourteen."

Joey thumped the table, rattling the plates stacked ready to be returned to the kitchen. Sienna recoiled from the foul curses turning the air blue. She would never have imagined the language spewing forth could come from mild-mannered Joey Lambert. Realising none of his vitriolic tirade was directed at herself, she sat back, admiring his fluency. She wished eight years ago she'd known even half the expressions she was learning today. Polite English just didn't give the same satisfaction.

She forgot all about being nervous.

Remembering his company, Joey pulled himself into line.

Mum would have washed my mouth out with soap.

Even his Dad minded his tongue around the house. He didn't regret his outburst though. Three grown men, and one little girl. Sienna must have been beyond terrified.

"I just hope they're in jail for the rest of their miserable bloody lives," he muttered, signalling Sienna to go on. "They are, aren't they?"

"No" trembled on Sienna's lips, but afraid of triggering another outburst, she changed it at the last minute.

"Get to that soon. That afternoon I took a short-cut across a patch of bushland, out of sight of any houses, so no-one saw them bundle me up in a filthy old blanket and shove me in the boot of their car. I think they injected me with something, because the next thing I knew we were way out in the bush with tall gum trees all around, and they were dragging me into an old shack. They laughed at me, calling me their little Easter present to themselves. One of them said they gave themselves a special gift every holiday. Made a joke of it. Oh, Joey. There were other girls before me. Girls who weren't so lucky."

The memory made her feel ill. Sienna jumped to her feet, grabbed the dirty dishes, and dashed inside.

"I'll be back in a moment," she called over her shoulder.

Her absence was longer than a moment. On the verge of seeking her out, Joey sank back onto his chair when she returned flourishing two cans of Pepsi. They cracked the cans and sipped the icy liquid.

"I'm not going to go into details, Joey. They tied me up and ... and ... used me. Till Monday morning. Easter Monday. They'd been tormenting me over what they'd do with me, but I knew letting me go wasn't an option. I wasn't the first girl they'd kidnapped, and none of the others had ever been reported as being found."

Joey turned white, and swore again, only this time Sienna stopped him with a hand on his arm. The horror roared in her brain, panic threatening to overtake her. The fingers on Joey's arm clenched hard. He'd have bruises next day, but the contact grounded her. She did her breathing exercises, restoring her self-control. Sitting up straight, hands clasped in her lap once more, she continued.

"Nearly finished, Joey, and I'm here. I did get away."

She took another sip of Pepsi, reminding herself that she'd survived.

"The plan was to take me out on a boat and feed me to the sharks. They said that's what they always did. If any re...remains washed up, there'd be no sign of foul play. Just a shark attack. The place we were was up in the mountains. Really isolated. They drugged me again and headed down the mountain to the coast, but they'd been drinking, and the car went over the side of the mountain and ended up in the bush at the foot of a cliff. Upside down and so crumpled I couldn't get out."

She stopped to moisten her mouth again. She was still fighting the panic attack, but it was easier now. She was almost finished.

"A motorcycle highway patrol officer riding by noticed the broken barrier, and stopped to look. Found the wreck, and called it in. They opened the boot, and found me."

No, Sienna decided, *Joey doesn't need to know more than that.*

He didn't need to know about the two days and nights she'd lain trapped in the mangled wreckage, listening to her abusers scream their lives away, one by one, until there were no sounds at all.

Until she gave up hope, believing she'd be next. That she'd die as she'd been intended to.

Until she'd retreated so far into the darkness within it took weeks for her to see the light again.

One day he might need to know about the claustrophobia which was a legacy of those hideous days, but not today.

"My kidnappers all died in the crash," was all she told him. "So, to answer your earlier question, no. They are not rotting their miserable lives away in prison, but they got what they deserved, all the same. So that's it, Joey. My miserable story. Still want to stick around and be my friend?"

The look Joey gave her said it all, but he put it in words as well.

"Don't be stupid, Sienna. Of course I'm still your friend. What sort of friend gives up when the going gets tough?"

"Not your sort, I guess."

Without thinking, Sienna reached over and squeezed his hand, interlocking her fingers with his when he returned the squeeze. A gesture she'd previously found one step too far, even with the few female friends she'd connected with during her university years.

"I need to do something. I need to move, or I'll go mad, sitting here all day replaying all those horrible memories. I'm going to go out to the falls and join the Tans and Gwyneth for that barbecue lunch. Why not come with me, Joey? We can swim. I've got plenty of food in the fridge."

"Yeah. Sure." Joey's affirmative answer sounded a bit absent-minded as he grappled with a whole new set of questions. Gwyneth.

"Sienna?" She looked at him.

"Gwyneth. Was she ... you know ...?"

"My gift from the gods to make up for all the horror? My one and only reason to go on living afterwards? My motivation to find the strength to fight back, to reclaim my life? A normal life? Yes she was, Joey. She's all those things to me."

Face flushed, Sienna lashed out passionately, fiercely, her words tumbling over each other.

"Without Gwynna I'd have given in to the blackness that enveloped me after the police brought me home. I wanted to die. I wanted it so badly, and then I found out I was having a baby, and I knew I had to live. For her. Mum and Dad couldn't understand why I refused the termination I was offered, but that baby, my Gwyneth, was my guiding light. I needed her."

Joey sympathised with Sienna's parents. He'd have thought as they had, until he heard Sienna's impassioned reasoning. He struggled to get his head around it. Until he brought that lively child to mind.

Whatever the circumstances of her birth, Gwyneth was a beautiful little kid. Sienna was a terrific mother. They made a perfect package. The frown that had creased his brow disappeared. He nodded. He loved them both.

"She's a great kid, Sienna. Who wouldn't love her?"

"Yes, well. But don't you ever say a word about her origins, Joey. Not ever. She doesn't need a burden like that. Anyway, let's grab some food and get going. I've had about enough of all this for one day."

More than enough, but what amazed Sienna most was how well she'd coped with telling Joey. It hadn't been easy, in fact it had been one of the hardest things she'd ever done, but do it she had. Without breaking down. Without bringing on a panic attack. Without ending up in one of her black depressions.

Maybe Joey Lambert is good for me.

At that thought, an unfamiliar warmth permeated her whole body. She sucked back a gasp.

Not going there!

11

When they arrived at the Rainbow Falls picnic area and Gwyneth came running to greet her mother, Joey watched with new awareness as Sienna, face alight with unconditional love, spun round and round, her daughter laughing wildly in her arms. It really, truly did make no difference to her that her child was a product of …

Face alight with pleasure and excitement, Gwynna ran to embrace him, and, happily lifting the girl into a bearhug as easily as if she were his little sister, Naomi, the last of Joey's reservations, his prejudices, fell away. Gwynna was just a kid. A nice, happy, affectionate kid.

As easy as that, her origins didn't matter to him, either. Gwynna was a child who ought to be judged on her own merits, just as everyone else was.

"I know you said you might join us," Elizabeth called out as Sienna and Joey walked towards her, Gwynna swinging and skipping between them, "but it's so late we thought you weren't coming. And look who you brought with you!"

Her raised browed signalled both surprise and approval. In common with the other women of Oxley Crossing, Elizabeth Tan liked nothing better than a good romance – one with a happy ending. Seeing what she wanted to see, that was exactly the outcome she anticipated for Sienna whom she'd taken under her wing, and Joey. It didn't matter to her that she'd never previously cast him as the romantic lead, Sienna's pretty blush told its own story.

"Grab a beer, mate, and get your meat on the hotplate, or you won't be eating till we're all finished." Geoff, less outspoken than his wife, waved a pair of tongs at the esky where a variety of cold drinks were chilling.

"Hi everyone."

Ignoring the beers in favour of a Pepsi, since he was driving, Joey waved to the crowd gathered around the picnic table.

There were more of them than he'd expected. Not only Geoff and Elizabeth and their two kids, but Geoff's parents and his cousin Lisa, young Bailey Tan's mate Jamie and his parents, Geni and Ben Wright.

A few minutes later, Megan and Jon Armitage arrived with their daughter Chloe.

Lunch finished, Molly and Gwynna pushed Chloe on the swings, while Bailey and Jamie started up a game of French cricket while they waited for their food to digest before going for a swim. Several of the adults chose to catch up in the shade.

Others, Sienna and Joey among them, joined the game.

Sienna, especially, had done more than enough talking for one day.

She jumped at the chance to avoid the women who'd all been at the dance the night before, and could be guaranteed to have noticed her abrupt departure, closely preceded by the sergeant's discreet departure with a handcuffed prisoner.

They could speculate to their heart's content, but she had no taste for answering searching questions.

When the Morgan family, whose farm bordered the Rainbow Falls Reserve, came down for a swim, Angie, who'd been very understanding the evening before, cornered her. Fearing the worst, Sienna was pleasantly surprised when all the older woman subjected her to was one very searching look followed up by a casual, warmly approving, comment on how well she looked today.

Joey, who'd drifted protectively closer when Angie, pretending to chase her toddler son, had made a bee-line for Sienna, took another look at Sienna, and had to agree. He hadn't noticed it happening, but she'd bounced back from the exhaustion following their long talk to a rosy-cheeked exuberance.

Laughing with the children, she appeared more light-hearted than he'd ever seen her.

More care-free.

Maybe making her talk about it this morning did help. Like some sort of cathartic cleansing.

His heart leapt joyfully in his chest, and he laughed aloud for no particular reason. Sienna had told him about her one-step-at-a-time recovery, and it looked to him as if she'd just taken another, vitally important, step.

From what she'd said on the way out, he knew she thought she'd taken all the steps she could, that a full recovery was impossible, but he reckoned she had that all wrong.

God, he hoped so. Otherwise his newly-discovered love for her was doomed. He was doomed. Because, if he couldn't make a life for himself with Sienna Smith, he didn't see how it would ever be possible with anyone else.

~~~~~

Not long after Barbara Morgan, matriarch of the growing Morgan clan, and Carol Tan, her counterpart in that family, had brewed tea, Sienna found herself fighting off yawns.

"Do you mind, Joey? I'd like to go home."

"Ready when you are, Sienna. I'll go round up Gwynna, and we'll be off."

They made their farewells, and climbing into Joey's twin-cab Ford ute, headed back to town.

It was as well for Sienna's peace of mind she didn't hear the speculation ensuing after their departure. More than one of their friends found Sienna Smith and Joey Lambert to be an unlikely couple, and didn't hesitate to say so. Not Angie Morgan though.

"I think they're good together," she asserted. "Joey needs someone he can take care of, and I reckon Sienna can do with a bit of extra care." She refused to be drawn further.

Elizabeth pursed her lips, considering the matter.

"You are right, Angie. I can see them together. I think they will be good for each other, like you say."
~~~~~

High-fiving each other, they stuck to their opinion.

Barbara and Carol exchanged smug glances, each confident they were one up on their friend Eddie Patterson; and that took some doing.

"We'll see," Angie said, but it was her husband, Alan, who had the last word.

"Joey Lambert in love. Bloody hell! That takes the cake."

12

Back home in Nymboida Street, Sienna stifled another yawn.

"Here you are, Gwyn," she handed her keys to her daughter. "Open the door, Love, then come back and help me with this stuff." She began hauling her cooler bags with the remains of their lunch from the ute.

"I'll give you a hand, Sienna. I want a quick word with you anyway."

Sienna frowned.

What more does he want from me?

Joey had been laughing and cheerful all afternoon. The life and soul of the party, but now he sounded serious enough to sink her heart.

"I've been thinking. That mob this arvo are all good people, but I reckon you ought to be getting to know some of the younger crowd as well."

"I guess. There are a few young teachers I work with, though, you know Joey. They're not all over thirty."

"Yeah."

Self-confident Peter Crawford, the young teacher she'd danced with, sprang into his mind, and Joey felt the nip of the green-eyed monster. He wouldn't be pushing Sienna in that bloke's direction. He knew Crawford quite well. Knew he fancied himself a bit of a ladies' man.

"I could introduce you around. Help you get to know more of the locals. If you like."

He looked at her expectantly, fingers crossed behind his back.

Relieved, he grinned back when Sienna smiled at him. Not her best smile, but a smile just the same.

"What would that involve?"

Theoretically, Sienna was willing. Unfortunately, theory didn't always translate comfortably into practice.

"Nothing too serious. Maybe a drink down the pub. A barbecue, if someone gets one up." He slanted a glance her way, pleased to see she looked interested. "I know you don't date, but it wouldn't be a date. Just friends keeping each other company."

Sienna banished her dubious thoughts. She trusted Joey to keep his word, and next time she was in company, she wouldn't be taken by surprise.

I'll do it, she decided. *I'll go out with Joey as he suggests, and think of it as a test.*

She was tired of being left out.

She wanted to join in.

Wanted to have as much fun as other girls her age.

Warming to the idea, she thought of the ideal event looming on her calendar. It was one thing to work with people, another thing altogether to socialise with them. She'd been dreading it, but with Joey at her side, she might enjoy it.

"That sounds an excellent idea," she approved. "And, Joey, why don't you come with me to the staff dinner on Friday night? I was going to go on my own, but it'll be so much nicer if you're with me. It's dinner at the Bowling Club. There are too many of us for Marge to handle at the *Victoria*, so the social committee booked the club." She frowned, nerves fluttering. "I just hope there's not too much drinking. I can't stand having alcohol fumes breathed all over me."

That was the second time she'd mentioned beer fumes, Joey noted. Filing it away for the future, he soothed her concern.

"Not with Ben in charge. I've heard if any of his people get out of line, he has a quiet word and they soon settle down. He likes to maintain a good relationship between locals and incomers."

"That's alright then. Oh, Joey. I'm looking forward to it."

Surprised, Sienna realised she was.

At the only parties she'd been to, ones that didn't involve family, she'd been a total failure. A real social misfit. But this one promised to be different.

No-one would be a stranger. No-one would expect anything of her, not even Joey. She could simply relax, and enjoy the company of people she knew and liked.

Today, the butterflies in her tum were down to excitement, not dread, as was usually the case.

"Righto. I'll pick you up Friday night. See you round, Sienna."

Joey sauntered back to his ute. Outwardly calm and casual, inside, he was dancing on air. He'd said they wouldn't be dating, but he'd lied. Friday night was definitely a date. Hopefully the first of many. Sienna might not recognise it as such, but he'd make sure everyone else did. Especially Peter Crawford.

~~~~~

On a quick trip down the street for bread and milk, Sienna and Gwyneth diverted into *Kit &Kaboodle*. A shop dedicated to clothing every member of the family, they found its variety absolutely fascinating. It stocked everything from practical workwear and Bond's babywear, to the glitziest evening dresses. Mary Oldman, in charge of the women's department, spotted them and offered her assistance.

"I've just this minute finished unpacking a fresh delivery, and there's a dress I think will suit you perfectly. Let me show you." She darted through a curtained doorway into the back of the shop, returning seconds later with the dress draped over her arm. "Why don't you try it on?"

"It's really pretty, Mum. You could wear it to dinner on Friday." Gwynna reached out to stroke a finger over the silky green and gold floral fabric.

"It looks like real silk," Mary added persuasively, "but it won't crush when you sit."

Tempted, Sienna felt herself weakening. Green was her favourite colour. It wouldn't hurt to try it on. Once on, she didn't want to take it off. The colours brought out the green in her hazel eyes, and the short, full skirt made her legs appear long and slender.
~~~~~

She twisted for a back view in the mirror.

Mum wouldn't approve. She'd say it's too short.

Anything which attracted attention to her daughter's beauty made Joy Smith fearful, but lately Sienna had begun rebelling against her old-fashioned, rather dowdy wardrobe. She'd discovered she liked looking pretty. Liked being in fashion.

A surreptitious glance at the price tag made her gulp. She wavered, until a second, longer look in the mirror made her rethink her budget. She could afford it, and, since it looked as if she was going to have a social life here in Oxley Crossing, courtesy of Joey Lambert, she needed more clothes anyway.

"I'll take it," she told Mary, before she could change her mind.

"You look really nice, Mummy."

Her daughter's admiration banished any lingering quibbles. Gwynna deserved a mother she could be proud of.

And she'll have one.

Determination to do right by her daughter had brought Sienna this far, all the way to Oxley Crossing, and continued to give her the strength to continue her process of liberation from the ghosts of her past.

~~~~~

Gwynna wasn't the only one whose eyes lit up at the sight of Sienna in her new dress. Face carefully made up, and strappy gold sandals adding extra inches to the length of shapely legs, she left Joey floundering as he searched for the words to tell her how beautiful she looked.
~~~~~

"Strewth, Sienna. I'll be the envy of all the blokes with you on my arm."

It wasn't all he wanted to say, but he was wary of scaring her into throwing up the barriers she'd only just lowered.

Arrived at the Bowling Club, Sienna felt Joey claim her hand as they reached the front entrance. Surprised, she was about to pull it free when she caught a glimpse of Joey's face. What she saw in it was so distracting she forgot she didn't do hand-holding. Joey looked distinctly uncomfortable, tugging at his tie with his other hand.

Damned tie. Shouldn't have worn the stupid, bloody thing.

Except that he wanted to look his best for Sienna. Make her proud of him. He'd even paid a visit to Thea's salon to have his hair and beard trimmed. He clutched hold of Sienna's hand to remind himself why he was here. In the last place he'd ever have imagined himself.

Look at you, Lambert, he jeered at himself. *Heading into the lion's den, and relying on a girl for a shot of Dutch courage.*

"Evening Sienna. Joey Lambert? Didn't expect to see you here tonight."

"Er, good evening Mrs Marsden. Didn't expect to be here." Joey tugged at his tie again. The flaming thing was strangling him.

Sienna shot a quick glance at him. He sounded nothing like his usual confident self. In fact, he'd sounded more like one of her Kindergarten class just now. Then she took in Caro Marsden's pseudo-stern expression, and realised Joey's problem. She swallowed back a giggle so as not to embarrass him further and gave his hand a squeeze.

Grateful, he squeezed right back, and took a firmer grip.

"Oh, I think we can dispense with formality, Joey. Most people call me Caro." Carolyn Marsden dispensed with the teasing, also, much to Joey's relief.

"Thanks Mrs Ma… Caro."

"See you later, Joey. There's Ben. I need a quick word."

Sienna looked over her shoulder, watching Caro Marsden bearing down on Ben and Geni Wright.

"Was Caro one of your teachers when you were at school, Joey?"

"Sixth grade. Not my finest hour."

"How many of the others here tonight were your teachers?"

"Probably about half of the older ones." He shrugged.

Suck it up, Lambert, he admonished himself. *Tonight isn't about you.*

"Oh, Joey. I'm sorry. I didn't think when I asked you to come tonight. I was home-schooled after … It didn't occur to me you might feel uncomfortable. But, you know, they're all decent people."

"Yeah, I know. Just that I was the class clown. Got on the wrong side of most of my teachers, one way or another. Don't worry though, it's all water under the bridge, as they say."

Sienna gave his hand another sympathetic squeeze and leaned against his shoulder for a moment. By then they were inside the auditorium and her friend Mandy Brock was waving them over to her table where she'd saved seats for them.

On his way to fetch drinks from the bar, Joey met Tom Creighton, his one-time science teacher. Accustomed to being met with a disapproving scowl, he was a man Joey usually managed to avoid.

"Lambert." Tom nodded. "Heard from Mark over at the Forestry depot that they're taking you on as a trainee botanist. Good move. If you need a quick refresher any time, give me a ring."

Struth!

A slightly dazed look on his face Joey watched Tom cross the room. If Old Creighton was willing to let bygones be bygones, anything was possible.

The meals were being served when a late arrival slid into the last spare chair at their table.

"Pete! About given you up, Mate. What kept you?"

"Good news, Thommo. The best. Hey everyone. Joe. Wasn't expecting to see you tonight, but I'm glad you're here. Want a quick word later."

"Well? If it's good news, share it round. We can all do with a dose of good news."

"Okay Mandy. You all knew I got engaged during the holidays?" Joey didn't, but that sounded like pretty good news to him all on its own. "Natalie and I are getting married at Easter, but she's not ready to give up work. Thought I was going to have to wangle a transfer back to Newcastle, only Nat rang tonight to tell me she's got a job, here in The Crossing, so it looks like I'll be staying."

"Oh, that is good news," Sienna clapped her hands. "Where will Natalie be working, Pete?"

"With the boss's wife. Geni and Megan are taking on another accountant so they can spend more time at home with their kids. Best part is, it comes with the flat above the garage, so I won't have to put up with your snoring keeping me awake, Thommo."

Conversation became sporadic, food taking priority over talk for a while. Which suited Joey, as most of the time his table-mates discussed work-related topics, unconsciously leaving him out in the cold.

"Bloody schoolies," Rick Bergman, a council engineer who was currently going out with Mandy Brock muttered in Joey's ear. "Get them together and all they can talk about is kids. It's worse than my mother's hen parties."

"They're not so bad," Joey commented with a sympathetic chuckle. "Got to expect it, Rick, if we want to spend time with our girls."

And spending time with Sienna Smith was very much what Joey most wanted to do. Thinking over Rick's grumble, he realised he was actually having a far better time than he'd expected. He reckoned he could handle more events like this. As long as Sienna was by his side. Under the table, he claimed her hand, absently rubbing his thumb over her palm. When she made no move to pull away, hope blossomed warmly within him. Later on, they held hands as they walked out to the carpark, too, and walked so close together their arms brushed against each other. Joey had expected Sienna to go on acting skittish, instead she was behaving perfectly naturally with him.

He couldn't see the nerves building up inside her as the end of the evening loomed. What if Joey expected a good-night kiss?

She wasn't stupid.

It hadn't taken long for her to realise this had actually been a date. She hadn't minded. Not really. If she wanted to be treated as a normal girl, then she had to act normally. And normal girls dated. Had boyfriends. She'd seen the admiration in his eyes when he looked at her, and reckoned Joey would be up for that.

The question was, could she carry it off? Not yet, perhaps, but maybe one day. In the meantime, she'd practise on Joey. One step at a time. She only hoped she wasn't being horribly unfair, using him like this.

"What did Pete want with you, Joey? You two were having a real heart-to-heart over at the bar when you went for drinks." She didn't really care, but talking defused the tension she felt building up inside her, now they were alone.

"Pete? He was sounding me out about joining the SES. Ben could have filled him in, but he didn't want to look as if he was crawling to the boss. You know, Sienna? I hadn't realised what a decent bloke Pete Crawford is when you get to know him. You were right about the others, too."

"Course I was right." She gave him a poke in the ribs.

"Teachers know kids grow up and mostly turn out okay. You were worrying over nothing. Don't forget, we have to pick the girls up on the way home. Elizabeth and Geoff are going to a wedding down in Coff's Harbour. No children invited, so I'm having Molly for the weekend. Since I knew it would be an early night, I said I'd pick her up tonight so they can make an early getaway tomorrow."

Sienna's nerves evaporated.

With two little girls along, she'd have no trouble bringing the evening to a safe close.

Joey's spirits sank. He'd been hoping the good start he'd made with Sienna would lead to even better things. Tonight. Not likely with Molly and Gwynna underfoot.

He was right. Sienna and the girls called goodnight through the screen door. With him on the outside. Philosophically, he shrugged, and headed back to his ute.

Tomorrow was another day.

THE MAKING OF JOEY LAMBERT

13

While Saturday was boringly routine, Sunday was certainly another day. Eventful in a way Joey hadn't anticipated, although perhaps he should have. In part, at least, because of his little sister Naomi's strongly expressed wishes whenever he spoke to her on the phone, which was several times a week. His mother encouraged all her children to stay in touch when they left home, and, since he loved his whole family, even when they were being bratty, frequent phone calls were generally a pleasurable duty.

On the Sunday following his date with Sienna, it wasn't the phone which dragged him from his bed on the one day of the week he allowed himself a lie-in. It was his mother rapping smartly on his door.

"Late night, Joseph?" She eyed him critically when he answered her knock, tousle-haired and still in his pyjamas.

"Mum! Was I supposed to be somewhere?" His mother expected him to fend for himself, and rarely intruded unannounced into his bachelor domain. Certainly not before breakfast on Sunday morning.

"Not at all. You can relax. I wouldn't mind a cup of coffee though, now I'm here."

"Yeah. Sure. Come in, Mum."

Moving an armful of textbooks to the floor, he ushered her into one of his pair of armchairs, put the kettle on, and dashed into the bathroom to dress. His mother was still sitting in the same chair when he came back to finish making the coffee, but he knew her keen eye would have taken in every last detail of his less than perfect housekeeping. At least he'd put his best jacket on a hanger when he got home Friday night, instead of tossing it over a chair. He slipped it back into the closet, whisking a pile of fresh laundry out of sight at the same time.

Marti's eyes twinkled as she accepted her mug of coffee and declined his offer of toasted muffins. Her Joey was a son to be proud of, even if he was only on nodding terms with his vacuum cleaner.

"I'm not here to check under the bed for dust bunnies, Son." Although she'd be willing to bet the ones she'd glimpsed would have disappeared if she came back later. "I'm on my way to church, and popped in to beg a favour."

"Whatever you want, Mum. You know that."

"I do, which is why I don't often ask. It's not for me, though, it's for our Naomi. She feels left out, with all her friends living in town and she's out on the farm. So I gave that nice girl you introduced me to a call this morning."

"Sienna Smith?"

"Any other nice girls I ought to know about? Of course, Sienna. I arranged a play-date for your sister."

If teasing Joey wasn't so much fun, Marti might have felt ashamed of herself, but his blush when he said Sienna's name spoke volumes, obviating the need to ask probing questions. Her first-born never had been able to keep secrets from her.

"I've just dropped your sister off to spend the day with Gwyneth and Molly. Those poor little Murphy twins too, I suppose, since they were tearing down the street as I came over here. Would you be free to bring your sister home this afternoon? It'll save me another trip to town."

"Sure. I haven't got any other plans."

"Good. Then I can count on you staying for dinner?"

Mum's Sunday roast? Affirmative to that. Saliva gathered in Joey's mouth just thinking of it.

"Since you're coming anyway, bring Sienna and young Gwyneth with you. I like that girl, and Naomi will enjoy having a friend to visit."

Joey felt his face heat up, and didn't care if his mother was playing matchmaker. Not when both their interests were so closely aligned.

Sunday roast and a date with Sienna. Life was about as good as it got.

~~~~~

Sunday dinner in the Lambert household was another occasion where the emphasis lay in good food eaten in pleasant company. An only child, Sienna found herself observing the dynamics of a large family with interest. How would her life have been different if she'd not been her parent's precious one-and-only?
~~~~~

Quite a lot, she suspected.

However, the more welcome and included Joey's parents made her, the guiltier she felt. Marti made her approval abundantly clear, and Sienna grew uncomfortable, sure the atmosphere would ice over immediately should the other woman suspect her son was being used. That no happy outcome would be forthcoming for Joey.

The worst of it was, Sienna didn't want to lose their liking and respect. It would be wonderful to be a part of this large, happy family.

Wonderful, and quite impossible.

She owed it to Joey to be honest with him. He mustn't be allowed to expect too much of her.

Which was why she invited him to stay for coffee when he drove herself and Gwynna home.

"I want Joey to read me a story," Gwynna demanded.

"Okay. One story, then. A short one," Sienna agreed, after a noticeable hesitation. Their friendship had progressed to the point she could no longer exclude Joey from entering her home, and didn't want to, she realised. She trusted him completely.

"Clean your teeth and get ready for bed. Joey can read to you while I make the coffee."

Leaning against the door jamb, Sienna listened to the tail-end of *A Fly Went By,* one of Gwyneth's perennial favourites.

Her heart clenched when Joey closed the book and leaned down to give her child a hug goodnight.

If only ...

While she went through her own routine of kiss and cuddle, she was aware of him standing in the hallway, waiting for her. The way her father had hovered while her mother kissed her goodnight.

Stop! Not going there!

Uneasily, Joey watched Sienna close her daughter's door with a promise to reopen it later, before she went to bed. His interpretation was not that Sienna didn't want their chatter over coffee to keep the kid awake, but that whatever she wanted to discuss with him was not fit for a child's ears. A conclusion reinforced when she also closed the kitchen door. She'd been subdued, moody, ever since they'd crossed the cattle-grid at the end of his family's driveway.

"Mum likes you," he said, deciding this might be one of those times when attack was the best form of defence. "In fact, they all like you. I overheard Paul and Tommy wondering what a smart, pretty woman like you saw in me."

"I like them, too." Sienna cradled her mug between her palms, staring unseeing into its depths. "As for your brothers, they've got it the wrong way round. They ought to be more concerned about what you see in me."

She looked up, her lips compressed into a thin line. Sad, not angry, Joey realised, his heart aching for her pain.

"Joey." Sienna sipped her coffee, putting off what she had to, absolutely had to, say; until it couldn't be deferred a second longer.

"Joey, we agreed we'd just be friends. That going out together wouldn't be a date."

Clutching his own mug, Joey nodded, not trusting himself to speak.

"Only it didn't turn out that way, did it? Friday night was a date. Even tonight was a date. It's not your fault. Please, Joey, don't think I'm blaming you. I realised what everybody was thinking, and did nothing. That makes it my fault." She gulped. This was harder than she'd anticipated.

"It suited me to have you to practice my social skills on. I used you for my own ends, deliberately made use of whatever you feel for me, and that was wrong. Now your mother thinks …"

She shook her head, refusing to put her fears into words.

"I'm not sure what she thinks, but it's a mistake. You mustn't like me too much, Joey. There's no future in it, and I don't want you to be hurt." Her next words were so hard to say, she almost couldn't force them out.

"I think it will be best if we don't go out together again."

There, she'd said it. It had to be said, but her heart felt ripped in two.

She's giving me the flick!

In a near panic, Joey replayed Sienna's words, trying to force them into meaning something else. Something that left him with a shred of hope. He loved Sienna Smith. How was he ever going to stand a chance of winning her love in return if he let her toss him aside now?

No bloody chance at all!

So he'd just better not let her do it. He got a grip, and chose his words carefully. Seeing her blink back tears, he took heart.

"We're both adults, Sienna," he said, feeling his way, "and that means we're each responsible for our own feelings. When I promised to be your friend, I did it with my eyes open. You were upfront with me, painfully honest, so you have nothing to reproach yourself with. I knew you had problems, that being your friend wouldn't be easy. Do you hear me, Sienna?"

He reached out to claim her hands, giving them a gentle shake.

"You've done nothing wrong. Neither have I. I really like you, Sienna. I want to help you. For yourself, not for what I might get out of it, so why don't you explain to me what you're so upset about, and let me be the judge."

"Oh Joey, it's not fair!" Sienna began sobbing in earnest, but when he moved to pull her into his shoulder, she straightened up, resisting his attempt to comfort her.

"I'll t...try," she whispered, sniffing back her tears.

"It all goes back to the same thing, doesn't it? To what those bastards did to you. You were an innocent child, Sienna. I don't hold any of that against you."

"But it damaged me, Joey. I won't ever be able to forget."

"It's only natural something as horrific as that would leave scars, Sienna. Even so, it's still possible for you to move on and live a full, happy life."

"No it's not. That's what I'm trying to tell you. Scars mean a wound has healed, but my wounds haven't healed. They're still raw and bleeding. I can't ever live a normal life, Joey. I can't stand being touched. Not even with affection. As soon as a man puts his hands on me, I feel a panic attack start."

Tears flowed silently down Sienna's cheeks, but she struggled on.

"Being held is awful. Even Dad can't hug me, and I trust him. I love him, and I hate the way he looks so sad when I pull away from him."

Her every word a dagger to his heart, dashing his hopes, Joey realised exactly what loving Sienna meant to him. It meant marriage, shared dreams and children. Growing old together. All the things his parents had, he wanted for himself. With Sienna. It couldn't be impossible.

He refused to accept it was impossible.

"But ... You told me about your recovery. One step at a time. That's what Laura's doing too."

"Yes. I learnt to shop. Go to the doctor. Take Gwyneth to preschool. Two years ago I was able to attend uni on campus instead of online. I thought I was cured."

Too agitated to sit still, Sienna began striding back and forth in her small kitchen, talking as she paced.

"Until I accepted an invitation to a party. It was okay till he took me home and wanted to kiss and cuddle before I went in." Sienna wiped her eyes and blew her nose. "I tried more than once, Joey, only it never got any better. Weird was one of the kinder names I got called. I finally decided to draw a line. I can be a friend, but not a girlfriend. Certainly not a lover. Or a wife. You deserve someone who *can* be those things. Now do you understand why it's best if we don't go out together any more?"

Joey understood, but he couldn't accept the loss of all his dreams. Desperately, he argued his point.

"Maybe you tried to do too much, too quickly. Those boys you went out with didn't know about you, did they? You just dived right in at the deep end with disastrous consequences."

Staring at Joey, Sienna felt a tiny flicker of hope. Dr Michaelson had said something similar at the time, but she'd been too upset to take it in, and, accepting her limitations, had refused to discuss it since.

"What do you mean?"

Fearful of making promises he couldn't keep, Joey was sure he was right. His cousin Laura had talked about a similar problem, and the way her counsellor was advising her to handle it.

"One step at a time, Sienna. It worked for all the rest, and I believe it will work for this, too, if you just give it a fair chance. I'm not like those boys. I know about your problems, and I can be patient. I can help you work your way through this at your own pace, one step at a time. You know, Sienna? I think we've already begun. We were holding hands on Friday night, and, once you got used to it, you didn't seem to mind."

He's right.

Her mouth a surprised oval, Sienna thought back. She'd been nervous at first when Joey had taken her hand, but she'd trusted him to release her if she felt uncomfortable. She hadn't, though. It had started to feel nice, and she'd been sorry when they reached the table and he had let go. It had still felt nice when he walked her back to his ute at the end of the evening.

The black cloud weighing her down let in a tiny beam of golden light. Greatly daring, a blush staining her cheeks, Sienna reached for Joey's hand now.

She felt callouses caused by hard work. When he curled his fingers around hers, she felt warmth flow from his palm into her own. Their clasped hands fit together. In Joey's hands Sienna felt safe. Safer than she had since she was a little girl.

If Joey was right about something as simple as holding hands, perhaps he might be right about other things, too. Although, ... No. She couldn't go there. She wouldn't think about being cured of her irrational phobia about being touched. What if she got her hopes up, and the experiment failed? She'd feel worse than ever.

"I ... I'm not sure, Joey. Holding hands is okay, but I think any more than that might be too much."

The eager light went out of his eyes and he seemed to shrink into himself.

Sienna felt mean.

Here was Joey, trying his darndest to help her and she was too cowardly to meet him half-way. She breathed deep, looking at their hands still joined on the table. They looked like a symbol of hope. Before she could change her mind, she gathered her courage and plunged in.

"It might be too much for me, Joey, but if I don't try, I'll never know, will I?" She gripped his hand convulsively, drawing strength from its solidity. "Let's try. Tell me what to do, and I'll try, Joey. I promise."

Yes!

Love surged through Joey, lighting him up from within. Impulsively, he lifted Sienna's hand to his lips, pressing a kiss onto the back of it. He could see her visibly struggling not to snatch it away. He loosened his grip, smiling at her when she let it lie.

"You won't regret it, Sienna. That's my promise to you. Together, we'll defeat your demons."

The blind trust he read in her eyes scared him half to death, but Sienna was his girl, and he wouldn't give up on her without putting up a bloody good fight.

"What now, Joey?"

Yeah, Lambert. What now?

He had jumped in with both feet, making promises with no strategy to back them up. He wanted … What he wanted were all the things he couldn't have. Yet. Not without scaring Sienna back into her shell just as she dared to emerge. *One step at a time,* he reminded himself.

"Right now, I reckon we quit while we're ahead. Tomorrow, after work, we'll take Gwynna and walk round to Mike Patterson's take-away for burgers and milkshakes," he improvised. "Let's keep it simple." Not that The Crossing offered too many date options to choose between.

"Okay." Relieved to hand over the initiative, Sienna giggled. "Sounds like a plan."

"So. Walk me to the door, Sienna. We'll say goodnight, and then we'll both dream of the good times to come."

Joey kept hold of Sienna's hand all the way to the door. Standing on the mat, he turned back to her and claimed her other hand as well. Slowly, giving her plenty of time to draw back, he leaned down to brush his lips across the rosy mouth which had been tempting him all evening.

He'd go crazy if he didn't get a taste of her sweetness.

Just a little nibble to see him through till tomorrow.

Joey felt the luckiest man on Earth when Sienna passively accepted his delicate kiss.

"Till tomorrow, Sienna."

He released her hands, stepped back and closed the door between them. Seconds later he latched the gate on his way out.

Fingers touching her lips where Joey's had been, Sienna watched until he was out of sight.

14

"No. That's no good, Joey," Sienna protested. They had just returned from their burger date at Mike's, and were discussing their next date while Gwynna splashed happily in the bath. "In the evenings I've got lessons to prepare, and if you spend too much time with me, you'll get behind on your assignments. That's your whole future at stake."

Frustrated, Joey ran his fingers through his hair. Not his *whole* future, but certainly an important part of it, if he was to achieve anything worthwhile. To have a future worthy of asking Sienna to share, which was now his goal. She was right. Her work and his studies were important. Only, if he had to wait till the weekend to see her again, he'd go crazy. Lurking at the back of his mind was the fear she'd change her mind about their agreement if he wasn't there to remind her with his presence.

"Tonight was fun, Joey. I don't want to wait, either, but we have to remember what else is important."

Sienna's smile wavered. Refusing to see him during the week made her sound like a school-kid who needed Mummy's permission.

Worse, Joey might think she was avoiding him, when nothing could be further from the truth. All day she'd been looking forward to meeting him, excitement fizzing through her blood whenever she thought about his kiss.

Which was every time she managed to steal a second to herself.

On duty in the playground at lunchtime, she'd barely noticed the children racing noisily about, intent on their games, she'd been so busy day-dreaming about being kissed. True, it hadn't been a very passionate kiss, but honestly, last night a passionate kiss would have been more than she could handle. Joey's gentle meeting of lips had been perfect for her first time as a consenting participant. It was clever of him to understand precisely what she needed when she certainly hadn't.

Would he know that tonight she'd be more prepared? More willing to experiment?

Instead, it felt as if they were arguing. Inspiration struck.

"Wednesday is half-way through the week. As long as we don't spend too long *talking* afterwards," she blushed, imagining what else they might find to do, "you could come to dinner here with Gwynna and I."

"You're on!" Joey's face lit up, only to darken a moment later. "Oh, damn," he cursed. "Can't. I've got footy training on Wednesday nights. There's no time to fit in dinner with you, Sienna."

He looked so utterly miserable, Sienna stepped up to him, laying a sympathetic hand on his cheek. His beard felt soft under her fingers. Softer than she'd expected.

Her fingers stroked, a miniscule movement, exploring the texture. She was standing very close to him, only a whisper of space between his shirt and her blouse. He reached up, his warm hand covering hers, holding it lightly in place. Sienna's breath caught. Her heart leapt in her chest. Looking up to meet Joey's eyes felt very intimate. Parting lips which trembled slightly, her tongue nervously moistened her bottom lip.

The sight of Sienna's pink tongue-tip sweeping across her lip offered a temptation no ordinary man could resist. More than Joey, who considered himself the most ordinary of men, could resist. With a groan, he lowered his head, catching that full, rosy lip between his teeth. Tasting. Wanting. Craving. It wasn't enough. Releasing her lip, his mouth claimed hers.

This was what he wanted.

What he hungered for.

What he couldn't have.

"You're kissing my Mummy."

Joey groaned again, Gwyneth's accusing statement hauling him back from the brink. He moved away from Sienna. Turned to look down at her daughter, standing in the doorway in her pink butterfly-print pyjamas, her hands planted firmly on tiny hips.

"I was," Joey admitted, his mind frantically searching for the best way to handle a situation he was totally unprepared for. "I like your Mummy," he stated, deciding to go with honesty. "I like you, too," he added, going with the flow. "If you let me read you a story, I'll give you a goodnight kiss, Gwynna. How's that for a deal?"

"Deal!"

Gwyneth, a more accomplished flirt than her mother, giggled, high-fiving him. Behind him, he heard Sienna turn a snicker into a cough.

"Fast thinking," she murmured. Louder, she instructed, "Joey's got to go soon, Gwynna, so go find your book."

In no time at all, it seemed, Joey was on the doorstep, having read *Where The Wild Things Are*, and delivered Gwynna's promised kiss.

Cupping Sienna's face between his large, work-roughened hands, he looked into her luminous eyes. The eyes of a woodland dryad.

"Goodnight kisses for little girls are sweet, but I like kissing Gwynna's mother best," he murmured, lowering his mouth to hers.

This time he had himself in hand, remembering what was at stake.

Remembering to go slow. Taking advantage of slow to be thorough. Being rewarded when Sienna's lips moved under his, meeting pressure with answering pressure. Returning his kiss, until he felt her withdraw fractionally.

"You'd better go," she whispered, reaching up to remove his hands from her cheeks, her action slow and controlled. Unpanicked. Her lips moist and reddened from his kisses, because he hadn't stopped at just one.

Joey blinked, his mind drifting back to their earlier conversation.

"I'll get back to you. Think about what you'd like to do on Friday. Goodnight Sienna."

He nominated Friday because he knew he couldn't wait an hour longer than that, but he'd be praying for Fate to bless him with an accidental meeting much earlier in the week.

His self-control skating on a knife-edge, Joey backed down the steps. Leaving while he still could.

One day ... he dreamed.

~~~~~

Astrology was a subject on which Joey Lambert had no hesitation in claiming total ignorance, but Fate smiled on him, leading him to believe his star must be in the ascendant.

A steady drizzling rain had persisted all day, welcome relief in the middle of a hot, dry summer, but not particularly conducive to outdoor activities. Joey's new job meant a later start in the mornings, which he appreciated, but it also meant the afternoon was almost gone by the time he returned home. On Tuesday morning he'd lazed in bed, reliving the evening before as he listened to the soporific patter of raindrops on the roof, then had had to scramble not to be late.

With no prospect of seeing Sienna, the wet day had taken on a dreary, grey aspect. Home at last, he'd showered, reheated one of the home-cooked meals with which his mother periodically stocked his freezer, and settled down to an evening with his latest assignment. Burying himself deep in his work, he completed a task he'd scheduled to spend at least another evening on. A hunting mopoke down by the creek the only sound disturbing the fresh night air, he realised the rain had stopped.

Stepping out onto his tiny porch, he gazed up at a clear, star-spangled sky.
~~~~~

Restless, and energised by a satisfying sense of achievement, he decided to go for the run he'd missed that morning. It wasn't late, and with the football season about to begin, he needed to keep fit. Thirty-five minutes later, re-entering town via the hill behind the hospital, he slowed to a cool-down walking pace so as not to disturb those neighbours who might be sleeping.

Which was when Fate smiled on him. Light streamed through the front door of the neighbour who occupied most of his thoughts these days. As he watched, she stepped onto her front veranda, a steaming mug in her hand. He angled across the street to lean against her gate.

"Hi, Sienna. Beautiful night, isn't it?"

"Joey!" she called back softly. "Have you got time for a cuppa?"

He didn't need to be asked twice.

From then on, Joey made it a habit to run at night, telling anyone who asked that he preferred the cool of the evening.

From then on, Sienna made it a habit to take a pot of peppermint tea and her favourite playlist out to the veranda for a relaxing hour or so before bed.

Without a word spoken between them, they'd solved the problem of making time for each other in their busy schedules. Of course, weekends were much easier since both of them made sure they cleared their desks by Friday afternoon, leaving two whole days free to enjoy each other's company, although they often had a gaggle of little girls trailing along with them.

Evening excursions sometimes included dinner at *The Victoria Inn*, under the observant eyes of a good proportion of the residents of The Crossing, which could be rather daunting.

For both of them.

More often they kept to themselves, barbecuing steaks on Sienna's back patio and watching movies together after Gwyneth went to bed.

Naturally, Joey wasted no opportunity to kiss and cuddle; Sienna a more than willing participant. Both felt excellent progress was being made to restore Sienna to a normal life. The 'one step at a time' rule appeared to be working just fine, and Sienna, appreciative of how Joey always seemed to know exactly what she wanted before she did, gratefully let him set the pace. A slow, gentle pace, with plenty of wiggle room to allow her to escape when she began to feel uncomfortable.

When March arrived, they walked hand in hand down the street to the hall for the monthly dance. This time it had been all pleasure, with no disturbing incidents to send Sienna into a panic attack. In fact, there had been no more attacks during the month since the last dance, which led them both into the mistaken belief they'd discovered the solution to Sienna's problems.

As their sexual experimentation intensified, Joey noted that while kisses and cuddles were fine, Sienna became uncomfortable if he forgot himself and pulled her into a too-tight clinch. Neither did she much like close body-contact when he was aroused, a reaction beyond his control, which, unfortunately or otherwise, occurred whenever he was in her company. The hard length of him pressed against her belly was a trigger which invariably led to her pushing him away.

As February led into March, Joey frequently resorted to cold showers.

Not that they did much to counter the frustration bedevilling him every time Sienna extricated herself from his arms at the very moment his hormones urged him to cast caution to the wind and make her his. Sadly, this unsatisfactory conclusion to almost every evening they spent together began to assume the proportions of a solid block of concrete barring further progress in their relationship. A block he could see no way around.

Sweet kisses and gentle exploration weren't enough. Had never been enough for Joey if he was truthful. Only his love for Sienna, growing stronger by the day, gave him the necessary self-control to remain within the boundaries laid down by her phobias. If he demanded more, pushed too hard, he was afraid he'd scare Sienna off for good.

Unsure how much longer his patience would hold out, he began employing avoidance strategies, such as texting to say he was snowed under and wouldn't have time to call in, or claiming he was needed on the farm on weekends. Which meant he had to spend one whole, sweltering day crutching smelly, recalcitrant sheep when he could have been swimming with his girls at Rainbow Falls.

Astute enough to realise what she was doing to Joey, whose presence had become necessary to her well-being, Sienna was consumed by guilt. He was so nice, always cheerful and amusing, always gentle and understanding. She'd lowered her barriers to him, only what if she never overcame her fear of sex, the most deeply instilled of her fears? Could never be a proper girlfriend to Joey? That was the point at which she always reined her thoughts in, refusing to indulge in daydreams of happy ever after. Unless she could sort herself out, there'd never be a 'happy ever after' to worry about.

I should never have let this begin, Sienna scolded herself, railing against Fate when depression struck, as it did all too often in recent weeks. After her initial progress, instead of getting better, she'd come up against a brick wall, with no way round it. It was so hard to keep up her optimistic front.

I'm no good for Joey. No good for any man.

Only now she'd had a tiny taste of the pleasure a woman could find in a man's arms, Sienna wanted more. Instead, she felt as walled up as Rapunzel in her tower, only Sienna's unscaleable walls were mental, not stone. She had had enough of being a prisoner to her own phobias. She wanted to live a normal life. Wanted to be free to fall in love.

She wanted it all.

With Joey Lambert.

She ought to tell him to find another girlfriend. But she wouldn't. Not yet.

She didn't even know how to raise the subject with Joey. Or maybe she didn't dare, for fear he took the opportunity to tell her he'd had enough. That she wasn't worth any more of his time and patience. Every time that thought entered her mind, her heart constricted, and a different kind of panic beat against her fragile self-control. She shied away from giving her feelings for Joey their true name. Refused to even contemplate the sweet, powerful little four-lettered word until she could prove her feelings to him.

If I was a nicer person, I would let him go, she argued. *Maybe I should leave Oxley Crossing, except, I like it here. If only I wasn't … wasn't what I am. A weirdo. A freak.*

If only I was a normal girl.

Deeply unhappy with herself, these sad, internal conversations usually meant her pillow had to be put out in the sun to dry the next morning.

How Sienna longed to be normal.

~~~~~

On the second last Monday of term, Sienna arrived home from work to find Joey waiting on her veranda.

"Hi Sienna. This arrived in today's mail." He handed her a roughly opened envelope from which she removed an invitation bearing her name along with Joey's.

"You knew Pam Lanner got engaged last weekend?"

Sienna nodded. Pam, a school-friend of Joey's, had attended the March dance with her boyfriend, Doug Morrison, a young stock and station agent from Gunnedah. Sienna had taken to her immediately, liking the other girl's earthy humour and pragmatic attitude to life on the land. Last Saturday morning they'd bumped into each other in Kit & Kaboodle where Pam had been excitedly showing off an impressive diamond engagement ring amid squeals and hugs of congratulations.

"She said they don't want a long engagement. I think the wedding is going to be in September."

"I don't know about that, but this is an invite to their engagement party. Her brother Ted is putting on a barbecue and dance in their woolshed on Saturday. You will come with me, won't you Sienna?"

Was this the opportunity she'd been waiting for? Her chance to resolve the situation with Joey?
~~~~~

If she could dredge up the courage to do it, there was one sure-fire method of blasting her prison walls to smithereens. One way to gain the freedom to be the woman she wanted to be. She'd proved to herself in the past that the only way to overcome her fears was to do what she was afraid to do. With Joey's help, she'd set herself free.

Excitement turning her eyes almost pure green, she accepted Joey's invitation.

"I'd love to Joey. I've never been to a party in a woolshed. It sounds the epitome of country entertaining. I wonder who I can ask to mind Gwynna? Nearly everyone I know will be invited to the party."

"Hang on." Joey pulled his phone out of his pocket and called his mother. Sienna stared at him, horrified.

"Joey! You can't!"

"Sure I can."

His mother answered, and after they'd exchanged greetings, he got straight into the reason for his call.

"... and Mum, you're always saying how lonely Naomi is. If you invite Gwynna for a sleep-over, Sienna and I won't have to hurry back early. You know how late these parties can go."

It was all arranged in a matter of minutes.

"Oh, Joey. It does sound like fun."

From being down in the dumps, Sienna grew more and more excited. Along with feeling more up-beat, she regained her confidence.

Damn it all, she lectured herself, *I will succeed. I will. I know this will work.*

On Saturday night she'd make an all-out effort to blast through that damned brick wall.

Pam's party was her chance to prove to Joey she was worth waiting for. Sienna was a bit hazy on the details, but she had all week to make her plans. Only one thing bothered her. She'd heard stories about Bachelor and Spinster Balls, and although this would be nowhere near as big an event as a B&S Ball, she suspected there would be copious quantities of liquor being consumed. And, since the smell of alcohol was one of her key triggers for a panic attack, she'd have to stay especially vigilant.

"There's going to be a lot of drinking, isn't there?"

Joey's grin faded. He knew how nervous heavy drinking made Sienna. Ever since he'd opened the invitation, he'd been making plans he couldn't afford to have derailed by one of Sienna's turns. He was going to have to stick really close. Then he perked up. Sticking really close to Sienna was exactly what he wanted. He did his best to downplay the less pleasant aspect of the party for her.

"Ah … As to that, the grog's bound to be flowing pretty freely, but they'll be a good-natured crowd, and I'll watch out for you, Sienna. Since you'll be with me, no-one will give you a hard time. We needn't stay late if it gets too rowdy."

He followed up his reassurances with a kiss promising all the things he had trouble putting into words. One of these days, he vowed, he'd tell her what she meant to him. Tell her he loved her. But not till he felt she was ready to hear it.

"Oh! You two! You're always kissing each other."

Gwynna, who'd come to see why her mother was taking so long, stomped off to help herself to an illicit handful of biscuits.

143

15

"It's not the flaming opera house, Sienna. Think Dolly Parton."

"Dolly Parton!" Sienna studied her own perfectly adequate but more modest dimensions and giggled. "You've got to be kidding."

"Yeah, well," her friend Mandy Brock giggled as well. "Rodeo queen, then. Boots and denim. Fancy shirt. Have you ever seen a woolshed, Sienna? Even all cleaned up and ready for dancing, it'll be dusty, and probably a bit rough underfoot. Wear those heels you've got in your hand and you'll end up with a sprained ankle."

When Mandy had mentioned Rick was taking her to Pam Lanner's engagement party, and Gwyneth was off with Molly for the afternoon, Sienna had solicited her friend's advice on what to wear.

"What about these?" Sienna held up a dainty pair of kitten heel ankle boots and a short white denim skirt.

"Better." Mandy rifled through Sienna's wardrobe, emerging with a black T-shirt with a jaguar picked out in rhinestones. "You don't get out much, do you? You've got nothing but work gear." She gave her selection another disparaging once-over.

"A bit ordinary, but it'll do, I suppose," she said, her approval lacking in enthusiasm.

Sienna wrinkled her nose, her lips downturned. A lacklustre 'bit ordinary' wasn't the impression she wanted to make on Joey. Or even the rest of Oxley Crossing. Mandy, replacing the offending garments, wrinkled her own nose sympathetically, then thought of a solution.

"Tell you what, Sienna. Grab your credit card and let's see what Mary Oldman's got down at *Kit & Kaboodle*."

Ten minutes later they pushed open the door. Mary, busy behind the counter, hurried up to offer her assistance.

"Hi Mary," Mandy greeted her. "Sienna's got nothing to wear to the Lanner's Saturday night. Can you fit her out, or do we need to make a dash up to Tamworth?"

Smiling delightedly, Mary ushered the girls over to the shoe department, asking Sienna's shoe size. If Sienna had nothing to wear, she'd start with the most expensive item to 'fit her out'.

"Here we are. Try these on for size. They're just the thing for a woolshed dance."

"Oh, they're perfect, Sienna." Mandy's eyes lit up at the sight of the calf-high cowboy boots in tooled pink leather. "Your white skirt will be good with them if Mary's got a shirt to match."

No problem.

Even with the khaki shorts she had on, the rose-pink satin shirt with its wide collar and fringed, lace bodice cut to a low V looked special.

"Joey'll cop an eyeful when he sees you in this."

Mandy laughed enviously, wishing she hadn't overspent her budget.

She cast a wistful glance at the rack the pink shirt came from, then fiercely turned her back on temptation. Spending Sienna's money was almost as much fun.

"It's not a bit too low cut, is it?" Trepidation added a quaver to Sienna's voice.

"Not at all. Have you got a suitable necklace?"

She did. She'd wear the silver locket she'd got for her eighteenth birthday.

Mary picked up a matching pink hat, then, shaking her head, put it back, muttering,

"Not at night."

Picking carefully through a display of costume jewellery, she triumphantly waved a bright pink, sparkly hair ornament above her head.

Sienna anxiously studied her reflection in the mirror, while the other two women animatedly discussed hairstyles, making her feel almost surplus to requirements.

"Are you sure this will be suitable?" she blurted out, interrupting an argument on whether her hair should be braided or worn loose.

She'd never worn anything like these boots and shirt, and was afraid of making a fool of herself.

"Yes!" Both women answered in unison. Mary, offering further encouragement, gave a quick glance over her shoulder to check for eavesdroppers, and lowered her voice to a sibilant whisper.

"I really shouldn't mention this, but Pam bought a checked shirt from this collection. If I know her, she'll team it up with skin-tight jeans and those two-tone boots of hers, and I happen to know of at least three other girls who'll be similarly dressed. You'll fit in, Sienna, no worries."

Allowing herself to be convinced, Sienna fingered the low neckline, realising that for the conclusion she was planning to Saturday night, giving Joey an eyeful might be just what she needed to get him in the right mood. Stepping back into the changing cubicle, she slipped out of her new acquisitions and into the clothes she arrived in.

When Mary handed over the carry-bag, emblazoned with her shop's logo, Sienna handed over her credit card with a flourish.

~~~~~

"You look great, Sienna."

Delivered in a voice uncharacteristically husky, Joey's rather banal compliment might have disappointed Sienna if not for the way his eyes had widened at his first sight of her, dipping briefly to the shadowed vee between her breasts, before riveting themselves determinedly on her face. Cheeks reddening slightly, he cleared his throat, adding,

"That outfit really suits you."

His physical reaction being everything she had hoped for, Sienna smiled, forgiving his lack of eloquence.

"You're looking pretty sharp yourself, Joey." It was true. Usually a bit on the scruffy side, he scrubbed up well when the occasion warranted the extra effort.
~~~~~

"We're both dressed Western style, but your black is a striking contrast to my pink, isn't it? We'll stand out in the crowd."

Taking her courage in both hands she went one step further, surveying him, very deliberately, from head to toe, and back again, pleased to see his cheeks darken again, confirming she was on the right track. She wished she was as well-versed in the art of flirtation as Mandy, but she was learning. Rising onto her toes, she placed her hands on his shoulders and leaned in to kiss him.

"Mmmm. New aftershave? I like that lime scent. Very enticing," she murmured, claiming his lips again. She'd almost said 'seductive', changing it to 'enticing' at the last moment for fear it might have been too much. She didn't want to scare him off.

Nothing loath, Joey kissed her back, forgetting they were in public view on her front veranda until a toot from a passing car jerked him out of the spell Sienna had cast over him. Nothing was going to scare Joey off tonight. He had an agenda of his own, and Sienna's unfamiliar flirtatiousness was the confidence-booster he needed.

"Idiot," he said, watching the car out of sight. He turned back to Sienna, her shining eyes and glistening lips tempting him to kiss her again. He resisted. Reluctantly. "We'd better be going, I suppose. Don't want to be late."

"Hold still."

Sienna plucked a clean tissue from her bag and wiped her rich, pink lipstick from his mouth, making an inviting caress of the slow swipe. Gulping, Joey took her hand and led her out to his ute, sparkling under the street-light. He'd spent the afternoon washing and polishing it. Concentrating on admiring his handiwork, he got himself in hand. It wasn't like Sienna to be so flirtatious.

So damned sexy, he amended, catching her eye with a sideways glance. A mirror in one hand and lipstick in the other as she touched up her make-up, she gave him a sultry, pouting smile that nearly sent him into the ditch. He sure as hell hoped she was still in this mood when he brought her home.

Balloons marked the dirt track guiding guests the half-kilometre down the paddock behind the house to the floodlit woolshed. The parking area was already full of utes and four-wheel-drives, forcing Joey to park way back in the dark. Hand-in-hand with Joey, Sienna picked her way carefully over the rough ground so as not to scratch her brand-new fancy pink boots. The pervasive smell of sheep overlaid by the inviting aroma of grilled meat and onions wafted from the cooking area to the side of the building where a laughing, chattering crowd had gathered.

~~~~~

As giddy as if she'd been drinking champagne instead of lemon squash, Sienna leaned into Joey's side, listening idly to his conversation with James Molinar. Football. She'd attended, and enjoyed, Joey's home games, and would undoubtedly go to others before the season ended, but she felt not the slightest urge to analyse every play.

She let their voices drift over her head, lost in her own thoughts as she analysed the play in a different game entirely. A game of her own making.

During dinner outside around the barbecue she and Joey had sat, sharing a haybale, their thighs pressed companionably against each other in the small space. It had felt good.

Exciting even.
~~~~~

When she'd deliberately pressed even closer, Joey had turned, catching her eye and planting a quick kiss on the sensitive spot below her ear.

In front of anybody who might have been watching!

Proof positive her scheme was working.

Not long after, the band had begun playing and they'd spent most of the remainder of the evening dancing. With lots of fleeting caresses and one or two more stolen kisses. Sienna's pulse-rate rose just remembering those kisses. If Joey had suggested leaving, she'd have been more than happy to. She wished he had, as the longer she had to wait to stage the final scene in her scripted drama, the more jittery she became.

Between dances, as now, Joey had stood at her side, his arm slung around her shoulders. One sight of that possessive arm tucking her close to his side had been enough to discourage most other men who might have been tempted to make a move on her. Which was fine with Sienna. She didn't want to dance with anyone other than Joey, especially as the night wore on and voices became slurred and feet unsteady as the level of beer remaining in the keg dwindled rapidly. Sometimes the alcoholic fumes breathed into her face were enough to make her gag. Thank goodness her lovely, considerate Joey, citing his responsibility as driver, was sticking to cola.

In spite of her campaign to seduce him before the night was over, the weight of Joey's arm casually draped over her shoulder was beginning to make Sienna antsy. His hold was becoming too tight. Too restrictive. Too possessive.

No, she corrected herself, determinedly refusing to let her fears take hold.

Not possessive. And not really too tight at all. He's being protective.

Maybe if she repeated it convincingly enough, she'd drive away the demons gibbering round the edges of her consciousness.

Protective was good. And she had to learn to endure being held, as long as it was Joey doing the holding. How could they make love without holding each other? And wasn't letting Joey make love with her the objective tonight? Sienna gritted her teeth and snuggled closer against Joey's side, slipping her arm around his waist.

She felt brave.

Daring.

Until his arm automatically tightened, holding her in place. Immobile.

Until, she breathed a sigh of relief, the band returned from their break and struck up a lively disco number from the eighties and Joey swung her onto the floor, releasing his grip to move in time to the music.

Then the music segued into a slow, dreamy ballad and Joey took Sienna into his arms. Their movement, along with everyone else's, became more of a swaying shuffle than a dance. Wrapping both arms around her, Joey left her with no option than to loop her arms around his neck.

Plastered against Joey, body to body, Sienna's breath accelerated. Her breasts were squashed hard against his chest. Unyielding as an ironbark fence post, his arousal jutted into her belly. This time gritting her teeth wasn't enough, so Sienna mentally recited her mantra to ward off incipient panic.

Succeeding, she consciously relaxed, rebuilding her anticipation. Joey wanted her, really wanted her. Her plan was going to work. She loosened her fingers to twine them through the curls on the back of his neck. His gasp, and the shiver she felt run through him gave her a delicious new thrill. A sense of female empowerment.

"Let's go."

Joey's warm breath tickled Sienna's ear.

"Ummm. Yes."

Thank goodness.

Sienna was ready for whatever came next. From a technical viewpoint, of course she knew what happened between a man and woman, but she had absolutely no experience of it as a consensual act. She'd long since decided to leave that part up to Joey, who'd never failed her yet.

Within minutes they'd made their farewells and were in the ute heading back to town, but not before Joey had taken Sienna in his arms for a long, toe-tingling kiss. He hoped to God her provocative behaviour tonight meant what he hoped it did. What it would if Sienna were any other girl.

The ute rattled across the cattle-grid onto the main road, and Joey pressed heavily on the accelerator, anxious for the end of their journey.

16

It all went according to plan, both the plan in Sienna's head, and the one in Joey's.

Joey had parked in his usual spot down the side of the Whitman's house. Seen by no-one except a stray cat slinking out of sight into a storm-water drain, arms around each other's waists, heads close together, he and Sienna made their way diagonally across Nymboida Street to Sienna's door, neither speaking a word. In perfect accord, as they often were, no words were needed. Both knew where the end of the night would find them. Exactly where both wanted to be.

Halting on the veranda, front-door key in her hand, Sienna, as was her newly acquired habit, turned her face up for Joey's kiss.

He didn't disappoint. He never did.

Joey took his time over the kiss, in just the way Sienna liked, savouring the delicious taste of his lady's sweet mouth and returning for more. He'd waited all night, all his life, for this moment; this pleasure; this night.

Joey refused to be rushed; even though Sienna's nerves were at screaming point, urging her to hurry up and *get on with it!*

Unlike every other night, however, this was not a farewell kiss. Tonight, it was a welcome home kiss. A welcome to the rest of our lives kiss. Joey lifted his head, smiling into Sienna's shining eyes.

Like magic, her nerves stilled. She turned the key in the lock and led her man over the threshold. She led him directly to her bedroom, with no hospitable offer of refreshments. Sienna was ready *now*. No way would her nerves stand the waiting about for the kettle to boil, for coffee to be drunk. Not when her scheme to tear down last barricade between herself and normal was going so perfectly to plan.

Anticipation coiling in his gut, Joey followed Sienna into a pink and white bedroom adorned with lace trims and ruffles. The scent of roses and lavender mingled sweetly. He breathed deeply, struggling not to simply grab Sienna and throw her down onto the patchwork bedspread. Looking around him while Sienna lit the tall scented candles standing on the dressing table, he began to feel vaguely uncomfortable. This was a room more suited to a young girl than a grown woman. The woman he ached for. The woman carrying a terrible burden from the past.

He truly believed he could help free her, with love and time and patience. Doubt crept in as to whether this was the right time. Whether he was the right man, despite the love for her filling his heart. Doubt as to whether Sienna was completely ready to take this next step forwards. They'd come a long way in what was surely a very short time, relatively speaking, even though to him it felt an interminable few weeks. Still, it was a giant stride in her one-step-at-a-time recovery program, from kisses to full-on making love.

Catching her hand, he drew her to him, anxiously searching her face. She looked almost feverish, hectic colour a fire in her cheeks. Her eyes glittered in the candle-light and she was practically dancing on the spot. Nerves or impatience?

"Er, Sienna? Are you sure, really sure, you're ready for this?" The last thing Joey wanted was to rush in ruin everything. For himself as well as Sienna.

"Oh, Joey. Darling Joey."

Sienna stroked his cheek, smiling mistily up into the face of the man she right that minute realised she loved. Loved, not merely liked. The fireworks in her heart put stars in her eyes.

"I'm ready. I love you, Joey Lambert. I want to make love with you more than I've wanted anything else in my life, only," she gulped as an icy shiver trickled down her spine, "only I need you to show me the way."

I love you.

Those were the only words Joey heard, and they reverberated in his brain, drowning out what came after. Sienna loved him. With a breathless whoop, he grabbed her with both arms hoisting her up against his chest and spun them round and round until they collapsed, laughing giddily, on Sienna's bed.

"Oh, God, Sienna. I love you, too," Joey gasped. "I've loved you since the day I met you, but I was afraid to tell you when you were so adamant a friend was all you wanted. Tell me you meant what you just said. Tell me it's okay for me to be in love with you."

Laughing, Sienna, sprawled on top of him, complied, punctuating her words with teasing kisses.

"I. Love. You. Joey. Lambert. I'm. So. Really. Really. Happy. You. Love. Me. Too."

Hugging, and laughing madly, they celebrated being in love, until, both gasping for breath, they sobered, gazing deep into each other's eyes. Afterwards, neither could have said who made the first move, but their lips locked in a kiss sparking a paroxysm of passion deep within them both.

Hands tore at buttons, desperate to discover the warm flesh beneath layers of disguising fabric. For long minutes on Sienna's bed, it was all heat and hands and mouths as they drove each other on. Shirts gone, they feasted on bare flesh, and when Joey drew Sienna's nipple into his mouth, sucking hard, it sent a jolt of electricity shafting through her body, lifting her off the bed. Flinging her head back, she cried out his name. Demanded more.

They'd explored each other's bodies before, but not like this. Then, they'd used gentle hands. Gentle mouths. Now they abandoned themselves to wild excess. Wonderful, exquisite pleasure.

Pleasure which exceeded Sienna's expectations a hundredfold.

She revelled in the tension building low in her body, coiling tighter with every touch of Joey's possessive hands, his every claiming kiss.

"We've still got too many clothes on."

Joey's groaned comment sent Sienna into a fit of giggles.

"We've still got our boots on," she whispered, not caring a damn for the state of the precious bedspread her grandmother had pieced together for her.

It was the work of mere moments to shed their boots and remaining garments, but more than enough time for Joey to reclaim a modicum of self-control. He wanted to make this good for Sienna. Good for himself, too, but most of all for Sienna. Wanted it to be an act of love, not the rutting of wild animals. With Sienna beneath him, his knee pushing her thighs apart, he consciously drove her onwards and upwards towards her peak. Pushing her further than ever before. Looking to go all the way.

The night was all going to plan. Perfectly. Amazingly.

Until it wasn't.

So lost was she in sensual delight, Sienna didn't see the horde of demons from her worst nightmares circling the outer edges of her consciousness. Didn't hear their excited howling and gibbering as they watched. And waited. Waited for her to be at her most vulnerable.

As Joey positioned himself to enter her, he paused to kiss Sienna again, briefly resting his weight upon her spreadeagled body. Pinning her to the mattress. Immobilising her. Trapping her beneath him.

Her demons struck. Without warning.

"Noooo! Noooo! Noooo."

Wailing, punching and slapping at his shoulders, pushing and shoving at his body which held her prisoner, Sienna, all recognition of where she was, who she was with, driven from her mind, struggled blindly to escape.

What the bloody hell!

Blindsided, Joey struggled to understand what was happening.

The warm, eager woman in his arms had changed in an instant into a screaming, fighting, panic-stricken creature desperate to escape. Rearing back, he made to take her in his arms, to calm her, only she was having none of it. With a final superhuman shove, she pushed him over onto his back, shooting out from beneath him.

Across the room she flew, until the wall brought her up short. Free at last, she collapsed, curled into a tight foetal ball, her arms raised protectively above her head.

Utterly gobsmacked, Joey sat up slowly, staring at the … the *thing* his lovely Sienna had devolved into. The thing, wailing with an eerie, unearthly keening that made his hair stand on end and his teeth ache.

What the bloody hell happened?

"Sienna?" Slipping off the bed, he crept closer, completely at a loss. What should he do, for God's sake? Nothing in his life had prepared him for *this*. He'd thought talking to his cousin Laura qualified him to understand what Sienna had been through.

Idiot! He silently castigated himself. *As if any man could possibly understand what violent rape did to a girl, especially one as young as Sienna was at the time. This attack is all my fault. I should have been more careful. How the hell do I make it right?*

"Shhhh, Sienna."

Crouching, Joey reached out, laying a hand lightly on her shoulder, springing back when she screamed and burrowed into the wall as if she could vanish through it like a ghost.

Looking down at himself, he cursed under his breath.

In the state she was in, the last thing Sienna needed was to be confronted by a naked man looming over her.

Retreating, he gathered his clothes, pulling them on any old how, one eye staying on Sienna who'd finally stopped that wailing, thank God.

Dressed, he approached her again, this time stopping a good two metres away, giving her space. Using the soft, soothing tones he'd heard his mother use with his younger siblings, he crooned reassuring platitudes.

Trembling, wild-eyed, Sienna watched him from behind the tangle of hair half-covering her face. Gradually, the trembling ceased and she lowered her hands from her face.

"Joey?"

The harsh raspy tone was barely recognisable as Sienna's voice.

"That's right, Love. You're safe now."

Gradually, she uncurled, pitifully attempting to conceal her nudity with her hands. Then, Sienna had exalted in Joey's admiration of her body, proud he found her beautiful. Now, she felt besmirched. Dirty. Ashamed to be seen like this, she turned her face away from him, avoiding the pity she was sure would be in his eyes.

This, at least, he could do for her. Looking around, Joey spotted her dressing gown hanging on the back of the door. He fetched it, draping it over her shoulders, careful not to touch.

Grateful, Sienna drew the robe around herself, glancing uncertainly at Joey once more.

"I'm sorry," she whispered. "Sorry."

"Don't be," he whispered back. "Sienna, Darling, tell me what you need, and I'll do it."

"Nothing. There's nothing you can do, Joey. You might as well go home. I need to shower."

Rising awkwardly to her feet, she scuttled past him into her ensuite bathroom.

Leaving Joey staring helplessly after her.

Go home? Not likely. Not as long as Sienna needs me.

Maybe she didn't need him, but she sure as hell needed somebody, and tonight, he was all there was. Wincing as heart-wrenching sobs rose above the sound of the shower, he finished dressing and tidying himself. Then he collected Sienna's cast-aside clothes, giving her pretty pink boots a polish with his elbow as he stood them precisely beneath the chair on which he'd deposited her neatly folded clothes. Her rumpled bed silently accusing him, he remade it, squaring the corners as if they might have to pass inspection. Switching on the wall sconces, he blew out the vanilla scented candles still burning on the dressing table.

With Sienna's bedroom restored to pristine order, as if denying the dramatic debacle which had occurred, he stood outside the bathroom door. Listening to the sobs showing no sign of abating. When he couldn't stand it a moment longer, he turned and made his way out of the room.

17

Huddled, a shivering wreck on the floor of the shower, Sienna, blue now the water drumming on her head had turned cold. Rousing, she reached a hand up to turn the tap off. Stiffly, painfully, she rose to her feet and pushed the door open, stepping onto the luxuriously fluffy mat which usually brought a smile to her lips.

Tonight, she didn't even notice it, simply reaching for a towel to dry herself.

Still shivering, she stepped into the pyjamas hanging on the back of the door. Picking up her dressing gown from where she'd dropped it, she pulled it on, knotting it tightly around her waist.

Catching sight of herself in the mirror, she reached for the brush and hairdryer to tame hair which was a riotous tangle. Wanting nothing more than to sink into oblivion and sleep, to wake and find none of it had happened.

Right. As if.

One sight of her dishevelled bed would bring it all crashing back.

Then, entering her bedroom, she wondered for a moment if she'd dreamed the horrible events which had sent her cringing under the shower. A nightmare. She'd had those many times, only rarely so vivid as tonight. So explicit. Then she realised.

Not a dream. Joey, bless him. He tidied up for me.

Sniffling anew, she wiped a tear from her eye.

He'd even turned the covers down.

Noticing the clothes on the chair, she picked them up, crushing them into a bundle. She was tempted to take them straight out to the garden and burn them, except that the worst panic attack she'd had in years couldn't be blamed on what she wore. The pink shirt and boots had felt wonderful on. *She'd* felt wonderful. Different. Besides, they cost a small fortune. Money she couldn't afford to waste. Stepping back into the bathroom, she dumped them into the laundry basket.

Casting a sidelong glance at the bed as she passed it, she wondered what Joey thought of her now. Her fit of the screaming meemies would have turned him right off. Worst of all, it was all her own fault. She'd been so certain she was ready she didn't listen to him.

My fault. All my fault if he wants nothing more to do with me.

She couldn't go to bed. Not even now it was all neat and innocently tidy. She'd take the tablets she loathed because they left her feeling so woolly-headed, and wash them down with a cuppa and bunk down on the sofa.

Yawning, she went through to the kitchen where the lights were blazing, even though she didn't remember switching them on.

"Joey!" Astounded, Sienna halted, staring at the man making himself completely at home in her kitchen. The man who shouldn't be here.

"I thought you went home."

"Nah. Couldn't just run off and leave you, Sienna Love. What sort of rat would that make me?"

"Obviously not your kind. Not that I'm calling you a rat. You're not. Oh, damn it! You know what I mean." She swiped the back of her hand across her eyes

"Yeah. I know." More unsure of himself than he'd ever been, Joey shoved his hands in his pockets before they reached for Sienna. He didn't think she'd appreciate his touch right then, and he wasn't confident enough to force the issue.

"I made tea." Stirring himself, he waved her to a chair and poured a cup, placing the steaming brew in front of her. "I found some that claimed to promote healthy sleep."

Slightly bemused, Sienna sat.

"Sienna," Joey's painful uncertainty smote at her heart. "I don't understand. What went wrong?"

Picking up the cup, she sampled the aromatic beverage, playing for time. She really didn't want to dissect what had happened, but supposed she owed it to Joey to try to make sense of it for him. Heaving a sigh, she took another sip, then set down her cup.

"What happened is, I had the worst meltdown I've had in years. Why?"

She shrugged painfully.

"I thought I was ready. I was wrong. Now I'm wondering if I'll ever be ready. Maybe you should give me up as a bad cause, Joey. We tried. We failed. Move on. There's no reason we should both suffer for my inadequacies."

Her lips were trembling and tears gathering by the time she ended her sad little speech. Having only tonight discovered she loved him, it hurt like hell to cut Joey loose, but she had no right to try to hold him if she couldn't even offer him a chance at a normal life with her.

Joey stared at Sienna, unwilling to believe what he was hearing. Shaking his head, he allowed anger to give him courage.

"You expect me to give up on you because the going just got tougher? What sort of wimpy bastard do you think I am Sienna? Give me some credit!" Tight-lipped, he glared across the table. "I told you tonight I love you. That means something to me. It means I've committed my future to you. Us. Tell me honestly, did you mean it when you said you love me, or was it simply self-justification for going to bed with me?"

Sienna's cheeks blanched; then fiery colour flooded back.

"That's so insulting! I meant it then, and I mean it now. I love you, Joey Lambert. Don't you see? It's because I love you I have to set you free."

"Bullcrap! I've always been free. My commitment to you is *my choice*. My *free* choice."

Anger shimmered in the air between them as they glared at each other across the table.

Suddenly Sienna began to giggle; and Joey's laughter joined hers a second later.

"It's not funny, Sienna," he gasped, "but I'm glad we've cleared the air. So, God help us, we're in this together for the long haul. Help me to understand so I can help you sort it out. Because I believe you can, Love."

"Well, I'll try. What happened to me left scars. They'll fade, but never go away. I have to learn to live with them. You know about the one-step-at-a-time. Dr Michaelson showed me I have to know myself to make it work. I have to understand the why of my reactions. We spent years analysing every little detail of what happened to me so I could alter the patterns that triggered my panic attacks. And it worked, Joey! It really did. I thought I knew myself inside out. That I could cope with anything if I tried hard enough. Only, I suppose because there wasn't anyone I cared about, loved, to motivate me to understand about the sex, it was still unresolved. I got blindsided."

"Okay. Then … Do you think you ought to go back to your shrink? You've got two weeks off coming up. Will that be enough time?"

"Time enough to make a start, anyway. I'll ask her to fit me in."

"Another thing, Sienna." Joey fidgeted, turning his cup round and round in his hands. "I think we ought to get married. As soon as we can. Then I'll be with you, helping you, all the time. Working together to sort out your problems."

Married!

Sienna gaped. Joey was racing so far ahead she couldn't keep up. She loved him, but *married*! That was a real big deal. She shook her head, trying to get her mind around the idea.

"Why not? It makes sense to me."

Joey had misunderstood her head shake, but as she thought it over, Sienna realised she wasn't any more ready for marriage than she was for sex. Now, how to explain herself to Joey without hurting his feelings more than she already had?

"I do want to marry you, Joey Darling, only not …" Then the words came to her. "Not with all this putting extra pressure on us making me all scared and nervous. When I marry you, I want to come to you free and whole. I want to be proud to be your bride. I want to walk down the aisle with my head up and see you looking back at me, proud as Punch. Can we wait till then? Please?"

A bit glum, Joey nodded. He could see her reasoning, but waiting was the last thing he wanted.

~~~~~

On Sunday, Joey had an away game from which he probably wouldn't return till late, especially if they won and went out after the game to celebrate. Pleading tiredness, Sienna wished the team all success then mooched around the house with Gwynna, too restless to settle to anything more productive than sporadically weeding the garden. Micky Murphy came and mowed, his sisters at his heels, so even Gwynna didn't need her company. By eight-thirty Gwyneth was tucked in for the night, and Sienna was dozing in front a movie rerun on television when something clicked in her brain, making her sit up straight.

Impatiently, she clicked off the movie she hadn't really been watching so she could concentrate on the idea which had just burst to life.
~~~~~

It wasn't that she wasn't ready to enter into a full sexual relationship with Joey. She loved him. She was more than ready to take it to the next level. Her mistake had been to arrogantly think she had her life under control. True, some parts of her life, she did. But sex was new territory. And it was the sexual part of the attack on her which had been the most damaging.

So damaging, she was nervous around strange men. So damaging, she could lose control, even with Joey whom she loved.

Grabbing a pen and paper, Sienna started documenting exactly what had happened on Saturday night, listing her successes and failures. Then analysing her notes to find the point at which everything came unstuck. Going back over them a second time, she made a discovery which had her punching the air in triumph.

That's it! All I've got to do is … Yes. Well. Maybe.

Coming down to earth with a resounding thud, she sucked in a long, deep breath. This was going to take a bit more thought, but she was on the right track. And now she had hope.

She didn't see why she couldn't make as successful a recovery with this as she had with all the hundreds of lesser battles she'd been fighting for the last eight years.

I wasn't wrong, exactly. I simply tried to run before I walked.

As Sienna went on talking to herself, her new course of action became clearer and clearer in her mind.

She needed to do a little research on the subject, and plan out her campaign step by step, but this time she would get it right.

She had to, or there'd be no happy future for her with Joey Lambert.

And that was *not* an option.

Not any longer.

Smiling to herself, Sienna packed her notes away and went to bed. Her mind relieved, she had no need to resort to her tablets tonight. Just Let those demons try invading her dreams!

18

By Monday afternoon Sienna had amassed a slew of articles on her research topic. Flipping through them brought a fiery blush, not just to her cheeks, but to her whole body. Burning with embarrassment, she hastily downloaded the lot to a secure site and deleted the links in case Gwynna came looking over her shoulder as she sometimes did. No way were these articles suitable reading for a child, although she itched to delve into them herself.

Her chance came a few hours later after she'd kissed Gwynna goodnight.

Oh. My. God. Hot and cold shivers ran up and down Sienna's spine. *I can't do this! What in hell would Joey think if I asked him to …?* Sienna's mind boggled. An interesting concept, *but …*

Not so long ago, simply reading these articles would have been enough to induce one of her panic attacks. To imagine *doing* … After Saturday night her courage failed her just thinking about it.

If *this* was what it would take, perhaps normal really might be one step too far. Her gate squeaked, and she almost jumped out of her skin.

"Hi Sienna. How you doing?"

Intent on hiding the evidence, Sienna stuffed the pages she'd printed off under the cushion of her chair as, flustered, she bounced to her feet.

"Joey. I'm so happy to see you. I'm so sorry I wasn't there to see you win, yesterday. I heard all about it from Mandy." She was gabbling, Sienna knew, even as she ushered Joey through to the kitchen with a guilty backward glance at the pages imperfectly concealed under her cushion. *What would he think if he knew what I was reading?* She blushed again. At this rate anyone could be excused for thinking she had a bad case of sunburn.

"Don't put the kettle on for me, Sienna, Love. I can't stay. With that exam on Wednesday morning, I need to spend a bit more time with my books." He took both her hands in his, gazing earnestly into her face. Looking at her now, it was hard to believe what had happened Saturday night.

"You really are okay, aren't you? I've been worried sick. Had to see for myself."

He'd rung at breakfast time. Apparently, he hadn't taken her reassurances on board. Sienna set out to assure him all over again of her present well-being.

"… and I've decided to get help," she concluded, deciding not to burden him with her crazy idea when he had an exam hanging over his head, the first since he'd left school. He looked anxious every time he mentioned it. Instead of causing him added anxiety, she ought to be soothing his fears.

"That's really good, Sienna."

"I'm hopeful this will all work itself out in time, you know. So you stop worrying about me and concentrate on that exam. I know you'll do well, Darling."

"Okay, then. I'm off." Joey was on the veranda before Sienna realised

"Hey!" she called after him, bringing him to a halt. "Aren't you forgetting something?"

"What?"

"This."

Sienna slid her hands up over his chest, linking them behind his head, pulling it down so their lips met. She might be too much of a coward to carry off what she'd been reading about, but it took no courage at all to enjoy Joey's kisses. More satisfying than chocolate, they were pure indulgence.

~~~~~

Humming to herself, Sienna watched her class settle down for their first lesson.
~~~~~

She sent a quick prayer of encouragement and faith out into the ether for Joey who would be settling down at the dedicated computer over in the administration block, the approved invigilator comfortably ensconced in the corner of the room. He'd be finished his exam shortly before morning break, and had promised to join her in the courtyard for a cup of staff-room coffee.

"To commiserate," he'd said, pessimistically expecting the worst.

"To congratulate," she, more optimistic, corrected him.

Moments later, her day was in full swing, but the happy mood stayed with her. Last night she'd studied all those articles again, thinking carefully about what she was reading. With the initial shock over, she'd been more objective, understanding what she needed to do. It was still super scary, and it would take tremendous courage for her to implement, but she could see the possibility of success. If she could pull it off. A tiny thread of excitement even laced itself through her trepidation. The whispered exchange she'd had with Mandy earlier that morning gave her yet more reason to hope.

"You're more experienced than me," she'd begun. "I'm curious what you think, Mandy. I've been reading …"

Briefly, Sienna had recapped the action part of the articles, leaving out all mention of using it as therapy. It had been disconcerting, but oddly reassuring when her friend had collapsed in giggles, her reply raising hot colour in Sienna's cheeks.

"If that's what you're planning as an Easter surprise for Joey, you'll blow his socks off."

"But, … I'm not sure I'm brave enough." Now it was Sienna giggling.

"Yeah, I know what you mean. It can be a bit scary the first time, especially for someone like you who's had a sheltered upbringing, but I guarantee once you get the hang of it, it's a game you'll want to play every now and then. And Joey really will love it, Sienna."

The bell ringing brought their confidences to an end, sending them off in different directions on playground duty. Mulling over Mandy's advice while she watched the kids playing hopscotch, Sienna realised two things.

The first; there was nothing out of the ordinary in those articles. Avoiding all forms of erotica, she simply hadn't come across it before.

The second; to other people, normal people, it was a sex game they played for fun.

Fun! Then she recalled how much she enjoyed kissing and cuddling with Joey. Maybe, if she found the courage, this would be fun for her, too.

Tonight, I'll open up to Joey. Let him have a copy. Then, after the holidays, I might be ready to try. One step at a time like every other battle. That's if Joey really does like the idea as much as Mandy thinks he will.

Fear and excitement, fairly equally balanced, played tug-o-war in Sienna's mind.

19

Tomorrow, Easter Thursday, was the last day of term. The school's annual Easter Hat Parade would be the main event in Oxley Crossing. Kindergarten, Sienna's class, had written a special story to be read at the start of the morning's events, and were practising their performance when heavy footsteps outside the door caused Sienna to look up from where she sat with the children in the middle of the room.

Rising to her feet, she approached the door.

"Mr Green! I wasn't expecting you."

Visitors were supposed to check in at the office, and Patty Morrison on reception should have called her, not simply let a visitor arrive unannounced in her classroom. Then her heart stuttered, her blood running cold when she saw what he carried, half-hidden, at his side.

"I've come to take Allissa home early." Tom Green looked past Sienna, to his daughter, Allissa Green.

"Get your bag, Alli. I'm in a hurry."

During this exchange, Sienna had edged close to her desk in the front corner of the room. While all attention was on Tom Green and his daughter, she flicked the switch on the intercom to 'send'. If there was anyone in the school office, they'd be able to hear every word spoken in her classroom. Speaking quickly, she alerted listeners to trouble before they tried to call her back.

"Mr Green. Please put that gun down. Guns aren't allowed on school property, you know." Her voice trembled almost as badly as the hands she clasped together in front of her. Breathing deeply, she strove not to give way. If she could hold it together for just a few minutes, help would arrive. She had to believe Patty was in her office, listening, and would send help.

"Please put the gun down, Mr Green."

"Look, Lassie," ignoring her plea, he swung the gun up so it pointed directly at Sienna's middle, waving her back when she took a step towards him. "Keep out of my way and nobody'll get hurt. I just want to take Allissa with me. Come on Alli! Don't just stand there. We've got to get a move on."

He spoke sharply. Urgently. His words reminding Sienna she had a duty of care to protect the children entrusted to her. A whimper of fear from one of them was a further reminder, if she needed one. She couldn't believe this was happening. This was Australia, not America. And Tom Green, of all people. She knew him only as a kind, loving dad. Then she recalled the announcement at last week's staff meeting. Jackie Green had left home with Allissa, and the courts had issued a Restraining Order against her husband.

Against Tom Green, who stood pointing a gun at her, Sienna Smith. In front of a room full of innocent children.

"Mr Green." Desperate to stall long enough for help to arrive, Sienna drew his attention back to herself. "I can't let Allissa go with you, I'm afraid." And weren't those last the truest of words. Firming her lips, she strove to keep her voice soft and reasonable. Soothing. "You need a permission slip from the office before I can let her leave school early." Bad choice of words.

Tom waved the shotgun in her face. Her knees were so weak it was a miracle she was still standing.

"Listen, Girlie. This says I don't need any damned piece of paper to see my daughter."

"Please. Mr Green. You're scaring the children. Put the gun down. Please." *You're scaring me too*, she added silently.

Stepping between Tom Green and the children, she addressed the class. "Children, please stay where you are and sit quietly. You too, Allissa. Sit back down with the others. Mr Green," she turned back to face the invader.

"This isn't the way to go about this, Mr Green. You must see that. If you take Allissa, the police will be after you, and it won't just be Sergeant Matthews who knows you're a decent man. There'll be special armed police, with roadblocks and helicopters. Everywhere you go. Policemen who'll shoot if you try to escape. Is that what you want for Allissa? Do you want to risk getting her shot when the police catch you? I don't believe you want to risk Allissa's life. Put the gun down, Mr Green."

"Of course, I bloody well don't want Alli hurt. She's my daughter, and I love her. That's why I'm doing this, don't you see? So we can be together. That damned wife of mine got a court order banning me from seeing my own kid. Is that fair?"

Not wanting the gun in her face again, his time she tried for sympathetic. Placating.

"It doesn't sound fair at all, Mr Green. Why don't you go back to the courts and ask them to reconsider? That's got to be better than this. Put the gun down and we can talk about it."

"Talk! Now you're beginning to sound like a bloody lawyer. Who's going to listen to me after this? They wouldn't bloody listen before."

Tom Green sniffed, dashing a hand across his eyes. His mood seemed to be changing. His resolution wavering.

"I might as well use the bloody shotgun on myself. Solve the whole damned problem."

"No! No, Mr Green. Think of these poor children having to see that. Think of Allissa seeing that. It's absolutely the wrong thing to do. Put the gun down and let the children leave the room."

"How would that help? As long as the kids are here, the police will keep their distance. They stay."

"But I'll still be here. I won't leave you, Mr Green. If you let the children go, I promise I'll stay."

He seemed to be considering the deal she'd offered. Sienna wrung her hands, trying to think what other arguments she could employ. She didn't want to be stuck in this room with a madman wielding a gun. She wanted to go racing out the door. To freedom. Safety. But duty dictated she put the safety of the children before her own, so she held her ground and tried a different tack.

"You know, Mr Green. The police are probably outside already." Mentally crossing her fingers, Sienna prayed he believed the lie she was about to tell. She had to play for time.

For the police to really come to her rescue.

"A security alarm dings every time someone comes through the gate, and Mrs Morrison would have seen you were carrying that gun. She would have called Sergeant Matthews before you even reached this room."

Not true, but if he believed her it might give her some bargaining power. Tom Green was just an ordinary, normally law-abiding bloke, not some psychopath.

If she kept telling herself he wouldn't shoot her, or any of the kids, she might eventually believe it.

Looking wildly around, he crossed to the windows, catching a glimpse of a familiar blue uniform as a police officer ducked for cover. Tom Green also ducked for cover, gun at the ready.

"They're bloody here!" He sounded as near to panic as Sienna felt.

"You said you'd help me, Lass. You better come up with a good idea quick-smart before the coppers out there decide to start shooting."

Does he expect me to get him off scot-free? No way that will ever happen. Not after he came into the school waving a gun around and threatening to kidnap a child, even if she is his own daughter.

Now she knew for sure help was at hand, Sienna desperately fought for control. With rescue at hand, she couldn't afford to get careless, only this was all so far out of her experience.

Then she calmed. No it wasn't. Different. Just as scary. But her life had been on the line before. She could do this.

"Sit down over here, Mr Green, out of sight from the door. And please, put the gun down. You really, really don't want *anyone* to start shooting. We can't risk innocent kids, Allissa, getting caught in the crossfire. If you put your gun down, the police won't use theirs."

She hoped she was right. She hoped there wasn't some gung-ho officer eager to make a name for himself by shooting the gunman threatening a schoolroom full of kids. And their terrified teacher.

"And just how do you bloody well expect the coppers to know if I put it down?"

Tom sat on the floor where she indicated, but he still clutched the gun to his chest, tighter than ever. His knuckles gleamed white against his tanned skin.

"I'll tell them."

"You're not going anywhere, Missy. You stay right where you are, where I can see you."

"I could write a note and you can send one of the children out with it. That would work. Better still, send all the children out, then they'll know you're sincere. Please, Mr Green. Sending all the children out is the best thing you can do at this stage. It really is."

"Tom! Tom Green. This is Don Matthews. I'm out here with plenty of back-up. You can't get away Mate."

Right on cue, the sergeant's magnified voice boomed out, reiterating Sienna's words. Inside, Tom Green wrapped both arms defensively round his head, the gun lying loose in his lap.

"Tom, be sensible. Put the gun down, Mate, and let the kids go, there's a good bloke."

In the silence following the sergeant's loud instruction, a child began to cry, rapidly joined by several others. A smell of fresh urine assailed Sienna's nose. For one ghastly moment she thought it was her, but it wasn't much of a relief to know at least one of her little charges had been scared into wetting their pants.

"Daddy?" In the fraught atmosphere, Allissa's tiny, wobbly voice sounded as loud as the sergeant's bellow from outside. "I'm scared. I want my Mummy."

"They're all scared, Mr Green. Let them go. Please."

Tom raised his head, tears filling his eyes. He nodded. Defeated.

"Okay, Alli Darling. Take over, Miss Smith. You win. I love you Alli."

"Sergeant Matthews," Sienna yelled through the open door. "The children are coming out. Two lines, kids. No pushing."

Not giving Tom Green time to change his mind, she marshalled the children. Leading the way through the door, she checked that no-one outside was pointing a gun, then stood back and let the children file past her to be met by the principal, Ben Wright, who whisked them off at a run towards the administration building.

Hesitating in the doorway, she looked back at the pitiful sight of Tom Green trying to stifle his tears. She looked outside. To where freedom beckoned, then holding back a frightened sob of her own, went and put a hand on Tom's shoulder. She'd promised not to leave him. It was time to live up to her word.

"Tom. Mr Green. Put the gun down on the floor. It won't be safe if you're still carrying it when we go out. Come on, now. Come along with me."

As obedient now as if he were a child himself, Tom put the gun down, took her hand and let her lead him towards the door. Going first, Sienna announced their intentions loudly.

"Sergeant Matthews. Mr Green is coming out with me. The gun is inside, and I'm not a prisoner. Mr Green is giving himself up."

"Righto, Ms Smith. Tom, I'll be at the foot of the steps when you come out. Don't do anything stupid, will ya Mate?"

Tom didn't, and in no time at all he was cuffed and stashed in the back of a police car with two constables to watch over him.

Shaking violently, pent-up tears finally streaking down her face, Sienna moved to one side, to allow the police access to their quarry. A breathy scream ripped from her throat and she almost jumped out of her skin when a pair of strong arms wrapped around her, lifting her off her feet.

"Oh, God, Sienna. I thought that bastard was going to blow your head off, and you just kept on talking to him, cool as a bloody cucumber."

"Joey!"

Sienna would have said more, except that Joey's lips, latching firmly onto hers, got in the way.

Until Don, shaking his head, turned his attention to Sienna.

"Lambert. Put that girl down. What are you doing here, anyway?"

Reluctantly, Joey let Sienna slide down till her feet were securely back on the ground. Keeping his arms around her, he spoke over his shoulder.

"Came in for my exam. I was mooching around sharpening pencils for Patty while I waited for the recess bell when I heard Sienna telling Tom Green to put his gun down. She deserves a medal, Don, for what she did, protecting those kids. Patty Morrison, too. You should have seen her Don. Calm as you like, she whipped out her phone and set it to record, called you and whistled up Ben and Caro to evacuate the school. Those sexist idiots who think women are weak ought to have seen our two in action."

"I wholeheartedly agree. Sienna, you were a real heroine this morning. Are you alright? He didn't hurt you?"

"No, I'm not hurt, but Sergeant, I'm no heroine. I was scared stiff the whole time. I just wanted to run away and hide."

"You didn't, though, and that's what true courage is all about. Switching on the intercom was a brilliant idea. That, and the recording Patty made are pure gold, but I'll still need you to come in and make a statement. No rush. When you feel ready. Now, can I do anything for you before I haul Tom off to the station?"

"No. I'll be okay. Everyone's being so kind." And indeed they were.

By the time she collected Gwyneth when the evacuated children returned to their rooms, and Joey drove them home, Sienna felt she'd scream if even one more person told her how brave she was. She, Sienna Smith, prone to panic attacks if a stranger looked sideways at her, wasn't brave. She was the biggest coward there ever was. The praise being heaped upon her made her feel a fraud. Made her feel she needed to earn her accolades.

"Joey," she caught at his arm as he was about to turn into Nymboida Street.

"I'm not ready to go home. I'll go now and get my statement out of the way. Drop us off at the police station, then you better get on to work. Mark Briers must be wondering what's happened to you."

"I can stay with you. Mark will understand."

"Maybe, but there's no need. If I'm as brave as you all keep saying, giving Don my statement will be a breeze. I'd rather do it now than have it hanging over my head. Come over for dinner when you finish work." She put her fingers across his lips, silencing his arguments. "Please, Joey. This is what I want. See you tonight."

Scrambling out of the ute, she took Gwynna by the hand, leading her through the gate and up to the police station door without a backward glance.

20

"Stop it, Joey!"

"What!" Startled, Joey, who'd just that minute guided Sienna to her chair, telling her to sit down and rest while he cleaned up after dinner, stared at her. "Stop what?"

"Treating me as if I'm so fragile I might break. You're even using the soothing sort of voice you'd use in a sickroom."

"I'm trying to take care of you!"

"Well don't! I'm prone to panic attacks. I've had a rough day. But I'm not going to fall apart if you treat me normally. I can wash my own damn dishes, for God's sake!"

Whirling back to face him after slamming a stack of dirty plates down on the sink, she caught the stricken look he was too slow to hide.

"Oh, Joey. I'm being mean, and you don't deserve it."

Sienna sighed.

Put her arms around him and hugged tight.

"I'm sorry I'm such a moody bitch. I really do love you, Joey. I just want you to see me as someone strong. Capable. Not someone you have to tiptoe around and treat gently in case I fall apart. Please say you forgive me."

"Goes without saying. I love you too, Sienna, and I'll always forgive you. But you said it, you know. You had a rough day. I thought I was being considerate. Sometimes, around you, Sienna, I get so confused I don't know how I ought to treat you."

"And that's all my fault. It's got to stop. It's going to stop."

In that moment, Sienna acknowledged what she'd been skirting around all week. If she wanted to be treated as normal, *she* had to act normal. *Be* normal. No-one else could do it for her.

"*I've* got to make it stop. Me. And I will, Joey. I promise."

She'd take all the adrenalin still flooding her system, all those testaments to her courage which had driven her crazy today, and use them to power her drive to achieve normal. And this time there'd be no backsliding, no matter how hard it might be. And it would be hard. Terribly hard. Her demons had had a very long time to become entrenched, and she didn't think they'd give in without a fight. Just look at what happened on Saturday night when she let her guard down. Determination flooding her whole being, Sienna looked up at Joey, making him a silent promise.

"Come on. Let's do the dishes together, then I'll send Gwynna to bed early with her iPad and we'll talk."

Then I'm going to sort myself out, once and for all. No more dithering and being too scared. I've got nothing to be scared of. Not with Joey.

~~~~~
~~~~~

"I know what to do, Joey. Theoretically. With your co-operation, I'll get it right this time. All those people today, saying how brave I am, and yet I'm too scared to break free from the dark place the attack left me in. Too scared to live my life. If I'm brave enough to face down a man pointing a gun in my face, surely I'm brave enough to face down my fears. That's why I want to go ahead. Now. While I still feel brave. Tomorrow I might be a scaredy-cat again. It probably won't be much fun for you, but fun isn't what tonight is about, Joey. What *I'm* about. *Tonight* is for conquering demons. Slaying dragons. And coming out the winner. If you're game to give it a go."

With a challenge like that, what could any red-blooded Aussie man do?

"I'm game, but you better give me a run-down on what you reckon we have to do to get you past your fears, Sienna. We need to work out a game plan, or risk another debacle like Saturday."

"That's easy. See, it's all laid out in these notes. I didn't think I'd be able to go ahead till after we've talked some more, but I've been studying this lot and I think, make that *know*, this is what I have to do. During my kidnap and rape," Sienna's voice wavered as memory threatened to invade the present, but with a quick gasp she collected herself and went on.

"I was completely helpless. Totally striped of all personal power. Ever since, my recovery has been about reclaiming my power. That's where I went wrong on Saturday, Joey. I wasn't confident enough, and in making you responsible for our lovemaking, I lost control." Breathing deeply, Sienna looked at Joey, willing him to understand.

"Until I'm completely confident, Joey, I *have to* maintain control. I *have to* be the one wielding power, or I'll fail. Look, this last article is so specific it's practically an instruction manual. Here, see for yourself while I go and tuck Gwynna in."

~~~~~

"Have you read it?" Nervous of Joey's reaction, Sienna had given him a good half hour to peruse the documents she'd tossed in his lap.

"Enough to go on with. Not sure it's going to be as easy as you make it sound, though."

"I'm not either, and it won't be easy, but I've got to try, haven't I?"

"And I'll be there with you, Sienna Darling. Every step of the way."

Damn right I will, even if it kills me, Joey vowed.

"Come and sit here, Darling."

Tossing the papers aside, Joey patted his lap. Over the last weeks he'd pulled her down on his knee more than once, but, too nervous, Sienna had never chosen to sit in his lap of her own volition, and was slow to respond.

"C'mon, Love. Sitting here is a position of power, isn't it? And giving you back the power stolen from you is what this whole exercise is about, as far as I understand it. You're in control. I don't do anything unless you order me to, right? So, c'mon, let's play this game. It sounds like fun to me."

A challenging grin spreading across his face, Joey patted his lap again.
~~~~~

Fun?

Sienna almost shuddered, but, realising the game she'd asked Joey to play had already begun, slid gingerly onto his knee; automatically reaching for his shoulders to regain her balance when she almost toppled off.

"Steady." Joey gathered her in so she nestled rather than perched. "You know I'd do anything for you Sienna, Love, only it really sticks in my gizzard, playing scapegoat for those animals who hurt you."

"No! No, Joey! Never!" Sienna sat bolt upright, refuting Joey's bitter claim. "You're nobody's scapegoat, especially not *theirs*. They're burning in Hell where they deserve to be. *You're* my saviour. *You're* the good guy. *My* good guy. It's loving you that's giving me the strength to fight to become a true woman instead of a shadow of one. Just like my love for Gwynna gave me the strength to fight to live an otherwise normal life instead of hiding behind Mum and Dad forever."

Urgently willing him to believe her, Sienna was lost in the dark velvet depths of the eyes scant inches in front of hers, where nothing but love and sincerity looked back at her. So close was he, she felt his breath warming her lips.

Without conscious thought, she leaned forward and closed the gap. Convincing him with a kiss more thoroughly than with words.

"I love you, Joey Lambert," she murmured. Letting her lips have their way, she showered his beloved face with exploratory kisses. "I want you. I really do, even if I'm a bit nervous."

Hands cupping his cheeks, her lips returned to his mouth.

Joey's lips met Sienna's with equal fervour, only, as her hands began feverishly kneading and stroking, first his shoulder, then his back as her body moulded itself to his, she shivered. Something was missing. Other times Joey had led the way, arousing her through the gentle touch of his hands on her body.

Then it clicked in her mind. Joey was playing the game, and it seemed he was better at it than she was. Smiling mischievously, she set about catching up.

"Touch me, Joey," she ordered softly. "Touch me the way you know I like."

The alacrity of his response instantly raised her emotional temperature to a point which made rational thought almost impossible. Made Sienna want more. So much more. She ached to feel warm flesh beneath her eager palms. Yearned to press her lips to the broad planes of his chest, presently barred to them by his neatly buttoned chambray shirt. Her Joey was way too well dressed for her liking.

If she wanted more of him exposed for her pleasure, she'd have to order him to undo those annoying buttons, or … undo them herself. She chose the latter, discovering an entirely new and quite delicious pleasure in the process. Moving oh-so-slowly, lavishing tiny nips and kisses on every inch of freshly bared skin, his moans and whispered exhortations informed Sienna her sweet torment was driving Joey mad. She was driving herself slightly mad, too. Her actions were affecting her as deeply as they affected Joey.

They had travelled a short way down this path before, only then, Joey's impatience had led him to take charge.

Now, his promise to play her game meant he couldn't.

He had to wait for her permission. Her command. Sienna let him wait.

Maybe it was nerves leading her into procrastination, but she preferred to believe her lack of haste was because she was having too much fun to allow herself to be rushed.

Smiling to herself, Sienna swirled her tongue round his flat, brown nipple, drawing it into her mouth and sucking hard. Joey jumped and hissed as if hit by a cattle prod. Sienna's blood surged in response, the growing tension coiling low in her body tightened a notch. She felt her lady parts becoming moist. Best of all, she felt none of the faint nervousness which she had come to expect when she and Joey were making out. Power, Sienna was discovering, was a wonderful aphrodisiac.

Somewhere in the far reaches of her mind, Sienna recognised the difference in her response tonight. Being in control made her feel strong. Powerful. Invincible. A woman. No longer a fearful little girl wanting something she knew was beyond her reach. It was heady stuff. And she wanted more of it. A lot more. Now she was the one becoming impatient.

She ran her hands over Joey's chest again, taking her time exploring the thrilling textural contrasts between swathes of smooth, bare flesh and lightly furred expanses. A man's body was truly a wonderous creation. As long as he was the right man.

Sienna followed the arrowing hirsute path downwards till the waist of his jeans blocked her access. Flicking a quick glance up to see Joey's eyes shut tight, grimacing parted lips showing the strain of being obediently passive, she purred. Flexing her new-found power, she pushed him a little further.

Unsnapping his jeans and easing the zip down, she slipped her hand into the opening, closing her fingers around the hard, straining length of him.

Once again, Joey jolted and hissed, sucking his belly in. And removed his hands from where they'd been kneading her bared breasts, stoking the furnace raging ever hotter inside her.

And left her bereft.

Bereft, and still too fully covered while her recent endeavours had Joey's garments hanging off him. Her ardour cooled and she sat back, frowning, mentally backtracking to find where she'd gone wrong. The momentum had been lost. Joey wasn't supposed to be sitting on his hands. He was supposed to be using them to make this exercise easy and, hopefully, pleasurable for her. She'd started out discounting any chance of enjoying herself, her aim limited to achieving the breakthrough she so desperately craved.

Then, fearless and in control, she'd felt that amazing coiling tension building and building inside her, and realised more was possible. Maybe. If she didn't lose her courage.

She wanted the more. So she'd better not turn chicken.

She wanted it all, whatever *all* was, and for that she needed Joey's active co-operation. Which, according to the rules of the game they played, entirely for *her* benefit, it was up to her to elicit.

Narrowing her eyes, she leaned in, caressing his body with her bare breasts, shivering at the tingle his abrasive chest hair set up in her sensitised nipples. Moving lightly against him, she kissed him, stroking deep inside his mouth with her tongue.

Releasing his lips, she nudged his head up to give her access to his neck where she could feel his blood pulsing beneath her lips. Tempting her to nip. A low, rumbling moan and a series of shuddering tremors informed her she was on the right track, but her nose itching from brushing against his beard, she pulled away. Just far enough to whisper plaintively.

"I'm feeling ever so hot, Joey Darling. I'm sure I've got way too many clothes on. Do you think you could help me out of them?"

"Your wish is my command, Darling, only, if I could make a suggestion?"

"Ummm." Sienna gave him another encouraging kiss and for a long moment he forgot what he'd been going to say. Until she readjusted her perch on his legs and he made a sound which was definitely more pain than pleasure.

"Ahh. Sienna," he whispered. "I reckon we ought to take this to the bedroom, don't you? We'll be more comfortable, and just in case …," he nodded towards Gwyneth's room. "Wouldn't want to be interrupted at a crucial moment, would we?"

"You're right." Shuddering at the mere thought of her innocent daughter wandering onto the present scene, Sienna slid off Joey's lap and, taking his hand, led him into her bedroom. Closing the door behind them, she looked at it a moment, then snicked the lock closed.

"Now, Darling," her smile aroused lascivious thoughts in Joey's mind of all the wonderful games they would play when *he* was in control. But it wasn't his turn tonight. Which was more than okay. *This* game was almost more fun than he could handle.

"You were saying you needed help to get out of those hot clothes?"

"Ummm. Then you can …"

Long minutes later, Joey interrupted Sienna again. Voice more than a little unsteady, he lifted his head from where his eager worshiping of her breasts threatened to send her into spontaneous combustion.

"You know I'm yours to command, Sienna Love, but," he warned, "if your wicked little hands keep *that* up for much longer, I'll explode. Won't be much use for a while if that happens."

Mind hazed with desire, Sienna's eyes immediately dropped to where her hands assiduously stroked and squeezed the hard shaft bared to her touch when the last of their garments had been stripped away. She gave it another greedy caress, loving the way Joey sucked in his abdominal muscles on a gasp. She was having so much fun she'd lost sight of her target. Joey was right. If she had to go back and start again at the very beginning, next time she might not have the fortitude to carry through to the conclusion. Even now she could feel her demons slinking up on her. The shiver rippling down her spine owed nothing at all to passion. Her body was primed for fulfillment but her mind was suddenly clear. And cold as ice.

Regretfully, Sienna marshalled her resolve. There would be other times purely for fun. Better times. Normal times. Tonight, she needed to stay on track. Mentally, she skipped through what she'd dubbed her 'instruction manual' to see what came next.

"Right again, Joey. Thanks for the reminder. Time for you to lie down and relax while I do all the work."

Giggling nervously, she patted him on what she considered a very nicely shaped derriere, giving him a gentle push towards the bed. "That's it. Stretch yourself out comfortably and keep those lovely big hands of yours out of my way." She'd miss their ministrations, but some sacrifices were worth it. Achieving normal was worth any sacrifice.

Only it was Joey who was being sacrificed. His kindness and generosity made Sienna's heart ache for using him so selfishly, and, stroking her hand apologetically over the body of the man she loved, laid out before her on her bed, she vowed to make it as good for him as she could.

Although with those bloody demons baying for her soul, she knew time was running out. More like a warrior riding into battle than a seductress claiming her conquest, Sienna clambered onto the bed, scrambling to sit astride Joey's thighs.

"Not much longer," she promised in a fierce whisper, "so just hang in there, Darling. Please."

The last word was breathed against his lips as she leaned forward. The searing kiss which followed, a sacred pledge.

There was nothing leisurely in Sienna's kisses and caresses as she worked her way down Joey's body, but anticipation more than made up for him what his lady lacked in technique. Joey had no doubt she'd succeed. If he could hold himself in check for long enough. Hands aching from the tightness of his grip, he clutched the sheet behind his head, determined not to sabotage Sienna's efforts by rolling her over and plunging into her. Which he so desperately wanted to do. Her tenseness showed how close to the edge she was, and a repeat of Saturday night was not on.

No way.

Trembling. Panting from the effort of clinging to the last vestiges of control, Sienna's progress was halted, her lips millimetres away from an obstacle she hadn't taken into consideration. She'd taken Joey's erect penis into her hands with no more than an initial qualm, but right now it was her lips which had almost collided with it.

Memories poured into her mind, sapping her determination. Memories of the vicious animals who'd abducted her forcing her mouth open. Forcing this part of themselves into her mouth over and over. Her gorge rose. Her throat choked up. And her demons, sensing her weakening, howled in triumph, stalking her like a pack of hyenas moving in for the kill.

Weak tears seeped from her eyes, blinding her, and sobs tore from her chest. Sienna could feel herself losing the strength to fight on. The pack was closing in for the kill.

"Sienna! You're doing fine, Sienna. Keep going!"

Joey's exhortations sounded in Sienna's ears, a clarion call rousing her flagging spirits, and she answered the call.

Snarling at her demons, she swiped her tongue along Joey's rampant erection, from root to tip. He arched up off the bed. Sienna's attackers had used this part of their bodies as a weapon to hurt, degrade and destroy her. But this was her Joey, who was all about healing and joy. Life. And the future. She dropped a soft, soothing kiss onto the velvety hardness. Her Joey's image a talisman fixed in her mind, she defied the pack. Eyes closed, she took him into her mouth.

Swirled her tongue around him.

Tasted him.

Knew him.

Claimed him.

He's mine, and I choose this!

Sienna flung well-aimed defiance at her demons. Snarling, still screaming threats, they backed off, conceding her a tiny victory. Still circling, they let her know she hadn't won the battle yet. With her strength ebbing again, Sienna knew her time was running out, and one make or break hurdle remained.

No time to think.

No time to worry.

To fear.

Time only for action.

Easing her mouth off Joey, Sienna rose up. Moved forward, deliberately sliding her slick female parts along the hard, silky length of his erection. Using her fingers to angle him correctly, she plunged down, impaling herself on his shaft. Felt him buck beneath her, his instinctive reaction almost breaking her resolve. The demons howled, closing in again

"Hold still! Hold still Joey. Please."

He didn't know how he managed it, but Joey held still. The two of them a frozen tableau for what felt to him an eon.

My choice!

Sienna felt the hot breath of the demon pack. Trembling, she commanded them,

Go! Leave me alone! Leave me with what's mine!

Miraculously, they backed off.

Further than before.

Then, when she repeated her command in firm, ringing tones, turned and slunk away into the darkness.

Fractionally opening her conscious self to her feelings, Sienna reached out. The sensation of Joey filling her body was wholly pleasurable. She felt like a woman. Complete. He filled her heart. Filled all its lonely, empty spaces with warmth.

With love.

A sense of wellbeing flooded through her. Excitement. New life to be lived.

None at all of the tearing, agonising dehumanising thrusting she'd feared for so long.

With each liberating discovery, Sienna felt her fears receding further and further, till, with their last echoes fading from her conscious mind, she felt free. Joyously free. Throwing back her head, she laughed.

"Now, Joey! What do I do now?"

"Ride me, Darling. Ride like the wind!"

Slowly at first, Sienna let her natural instincts take over. Soon her movements quickened, and with Joey's hands on her hips, guiding her, she rode. It was heat and speed, wild and free, from the fires of her personal Hell into the halls of Valhalla, collapsing at last as the stars exploded around them.

21

"Oh Shit!" Muttering expletives under his breath, Joey sat up against the bedhead, pulling Sienna, sobbing, into his arms. Just when he'd thought they were home free! Seemed in his jubilant euphoria he'd got ahead of himself.

"Shush, Sienna. I'm sorry, Love. So sorry." Rubbing her back in a calming motion, he whispered his contrition over and over while silently cursing himself for failing her at the ultimate moment in her struggle. A struggle which had meant so much to both of them.

"It's okay. I'm okay, Darling. All okay." Releasing a hand from Joey's enveloping embrace, Sienna patted him on the cheek. "It's okay," she sniffled, swallowing back her sobs. Freeing her other hand, she slipped her arms around her lover's neck, lifting her tearstained face to him.

It wasn't till Joey saw her radiant smile shining through her tears, a rainbow after the storm, that his heart slowed its frantic pounding.

"We did it, Joey! We did it!" Sienna bounced in his arms, unable to stay still.

"When I saw you crying, I thought I'd blown it."

"I almost did. Without you keeping me on track, I couldn't have done it. You were wonderful, Joey. Absolutely wonderful." Almost as an afterthought, she added a reassuring, "The tears are just a reaction. Relief. Something like that."

"Thank God for that. I thought you were freaking out. You know, Sienna? I wasn't sure it would work, just that if it was to have any chance at all, then I had to support you. One hundred percent. You were bloody amazing."

"*We* were bloody amazing, Joey." Sienna corrected, stifling a yawn. "I can't believe how utterly exhausted I feel, now it's over."

As trusting as a child, she curled up against his side and closed her eyes. Watching her fall asleep, Joey had no difficulty believing. Yawning himself, he realised Sienna wasn't the only one suffering from exhaustion. He supposed he ought to go home, but he was so warm and comfortable in Sienna's bed. What if she woke to a panic attack in the middle of the night? Still rationalising his decision to stay, he drifted into sleep, his arm holding Sienna spooned into the protective curve of his body.

The kookaburras were heralding the piccaninny dawn when, waking simultaneously, Joey and Sienna reached for each other. This time their lovemaking was sweet and gentle.

Building steadily to a long, rolling climax, it was satisfying in an entirely different way to the wild ride of the night before. At the last moment, Joey had flipped onto his back, lifting Sienna on top.

"Don't want to take any chances," he murmured, "besides, I like the view." Sienna's answering giggle, assuring him her cure was permanent, rang in his ears. A peal of Heavenly bells, promising a bright future.

Warm and sated, they dozed again until Sienna's alarm roused them to full wakefulness a short time later. Yawning, Joey stretched and, unfazed by his nudity, rolled out of bed in one fluid movement. Bending, he gathered his clothes from the floor and began dressing.

Propping herself lazily against the headboard, Sienna pulled the covers up to her neck, watching him. It was incredible to think how short a time ago the sight of a naked man in her bedroom would have sent her into panic mode. Now … She smiled, a sensuous, feline smile, admiring the view reflected front and back in the mirrored doors of her wardrobe.

Catching sight of her in the mirror, Joey zipped his jeans, turned, and, a wolfish grin sending Sienna's pulse racing in expectation, reached her in two quick strides. Scooping her onto his lap, he claimed a kiss that left both of them craving for more.

"Pity there's no time. With the Easter long weekend starting tomorrow, Mark's got a list a mile long of things that need doing, so I can't afford to be late."

"Me too. Gwynna and I are supposed to be leaving this afternoon and I haven't even started packing."

"Wish you weren't going."

"Umm. Me too."

"Seriously, though, Sienna. There's no reason to wait, now, is there?"

Bewildered, Sienna interrogated Joey with one delicately raised brow. Had she missed an important part of the conversation?

"You know." Blushing, Joey elaborated. "Getting married. You've dropkicked your demons out of the park, so now there's no reason we have to wait. Is there?" By now he was sounding a bit anxious.

"Do I detect a proposal somewhere in there, Darling?" Teasing Joey was fun, but seeing his blush deepen, Sienna relented, her smile saying it all.

"Yeah. But I'll say it properly. Sienna Smith, Darling, will you put me out of my misery and say you'll marry me?"

"I will, Joey. Oh, yes, I'll marry you. I'll be yours forever."

"Yes!"

Celebrating, they almost forgot they both had places to go.

"Mum! Are you awake?"

Springing off the bed, Sienna grabbed her robe and slipped out the door, hissing at Joey to wait till the coast was clear.

"I'm awake, Gwynna. Why don't you go back to your room and get dressed? I'll have my shower, then make breakfast."

"I'll ring you at lunchtime," Joey whispered, stealing another kiss as he tiptoed out.

"I'll be waiting," Sienna whispered back, "but, Darling, would you like to have breakfast with us? We won't have much time together before Gwynna and I leave. I want to make the most of every moment."

"I'll be here."

The sound of a door slamming reminded them not to dally. Sienna eased the front door shut behind Joey then dashed for the shower. Then dashed back out again before she'd even switched on the taps, scooping her phone up from the bedside table. Crossing her fingers for luck, she pressed the call button.

~~~~~

Breakfast over, Gwyneth ran out into the back garden to give the bacon rinds to the magpies. Seizing his opportunity, Joey reached into his pocket, bringing out an old, blue-velvet ring box.

"Sienna Love, my Gran's been sharing out her treasures while she can still enjoy herself doing it. She gave me this. Said it was for the woman I loved. That's you." Smiling, he laid a quick kiss on the soft, pink lips he couldn't get enough of.
~~~~~

"It's not an engagement ring, Sienna. I'll buy you one of those as soon as possible, but Gramps gave it to Gran when they were courting. Will you wear it for me?"

He opened the box, showing her an antique Victorian ring on which the initial letters of the square-cut stones - diamond, emerald, amethyst, ruby, another emerald, a sapphire and a topaz - spelt the word 'dearest'. Catching the sun, the stones flashed their colours. Sienna had heard of these romantic rings, but had never seen one.

"Oh. Oh Joey. It's lovely. I'll be proud to wear it."

She held out her left hand, and Joey slid the ring onto her fourth finger.

"It fits, Joey. Oh, Darling, I'm meant to wear it. I'm not swapping this beautiful ring which has been given in love more than once for any cold, new diamond. This is all the engagement ring I want."

"Are you two kissing again? Every time I turn round you're kissing Joey, Mum."

They moved apart reluctantly at Gwynna's truculent interruption. Dropping to his haunches in front of the child, Joey took her hands in his.

"Gwyneth, I've got something serious to ask you. I love your Mum, and she loves me. We want to get married, and we'd really like you to be happy for us." He'd have said more, only he never got the chance.

"Married! You and Mum?" Gwynna's squeal could have been heard across the other side of Morgan's Creek. "When? Can I be a bridesmaid? Can I Mum?"

"Of course you …" Sienna began. Before she completed her sentence, her daughter, eager to share the good news, dashed out the door to where their neighbour was cutting roses from the bushes alongside the low fence dividing the houses.

"Aunt Eddie! Aunt Eddie! Mum and Joey are getting married! I can't wait to tell everyone at school."

"I guess she approves," Sienna laughed, linking her arm through Joey's and following her daughter outside. Glancing significantly at the recipient of Gwynna's confidences, she added, "You'd better call your parents before the news spreads any further."

Amid the flurry of congratulations which ensued, Joey leaned down to kiss Eddie's cheek.

"Trust you to be first with the news as usual, Eddie." Straightening, he turned to Sienna. "Gotta go. Bye Darling. Bye Kid. I'll call Mum on the way." With another round of kisses, he was on his way.

It wasn't until he was gone, Sienna realised she hadn't told him about the call she'd made. No matter. It could wait till later. By then she might have an answer from her mother.

~~~~~
~~~~~

The last day of school before Easter was always fun, but this time, after the dramatic and frightening events of the day before, it was especially so. In actual fact, so much else had happened, Sienna had forgotten about Tom Green until colleagues and parents began asking how she was. Thanks to Gwynna, news of her engagement swept through the school like wildfire, happy news bringing smiles back to a lot of faces which had started the day on a sombre note.

After the dress-up parade, Sienna, in the rabbit onesies she'd donned in the spirit of the day, was presented with a huge bouquet of roses looking suspiciously like the ones growing next door in Eddie Patterson's garden, and wished all the best from the whole school community. Bubbling over with joy, she excused herself when her phone played its signature tune.

"Joey," she answered. "I'm so glad you rang. Did you tell your parents?"

"I did. Mum's over the moon. Her screech was almost as deafening as Gwynna's. Dad was a bit calmer, but I could tell he's pleased. They both like you, you know. Mum reckons marrying you will be the making of me."

"That's so nice of her, but I hope you told them I don't want to change a single thing about you. I love you exactly as you are. But, Joey. I rang my parents too. As you can imagine, because they don't know you, they're happy for me, but a bit uptight at the same time. So ... I suggested they come to The Crossing for Easter instead of Gwynna and I going to them. They agreed, Joey! They'll get here tomorrow morning, so will you come to lunch and get to know them?"

Tugging at the neck of his collar, Joey accepted the invitation. If he'd had a tie, he'd have had to loosen it. Being put through his paces by Sienna's father, Gary Smith, wasn't something he looked forward to, but he was careful not to let Sienna know how nervous he felt.

"I'll let Mum know. She'll want them to spend some time out at the farm while they're here."

"Why don't you let me do that? I'd like our two families to really get to know each other. Your Mum and I can co-ordinate events.

In the end, the weekend went swimmingly, both sets of parents finding plenty of common ground. A miracle organiser, Marti Lambert hosted an engagement party barbecue on Easter Monday attended by as many family and friends as could make it at short notice. Tipsy with excitement, Gwyneth and Naomi stole the show when they got up together to propose a toast.

"... and," Naomi concluded, "it's really amazing, you know. When my big brother marries Gwynna's Mum, that will make me Gwynna's auntie. You'll have to call me Aunt Naomi, Gwynn."

"Aunt Naomi! That's so funny," Gwynna giggled, jumping up and down. "And, guess what else? I get a new Daddy, and a new Grandma and Grandpoppy too! I'm so lucky."

Epilogue

At exactly two o'clock in the afternoon on the first Saturday in July, at the end of Term Two, Poppy MacIntosh, the organist launched into The Bridal March. Reverend Charles, smiling benignly, took his place in front of the altar. Joey Lambert and his brother Noah stood, Joey fidgeting with his tie while glancing over his shoulder towards the entrance to the nave. The congregation, filling the small church to overflowing, fell into a hushed silence.

Then Clarice and Estelle Murphy, looking like fairy princesses in identical emerald dresses and floral wreaths on their blonde hair, led the procession into the church. Each of them carried a basket of flowers which Eddie Patterson unobtrusively directed them to place on the floor at either end of the altar.

Five metres behind the twins came Molly Tan, similarly attired in rich topaz. Then, at a further five metres, Naomi Lambert in sapphire blue, bearing two more baskets of flowers to dress the top of the altar.

An amethyst fairy, Gwyneth Smith carried a white satin and lace heart shaped cushion to which the wedding rings were securely attached.

In a deceptively simple long, ruby sheath, Mandy Brock followed the bevy of little girls, a bouquet of Pierre de Ronsard roses in her hands.

Somewhere a quickly hushed voiced whispered loudly, "See, Mum. They're the colours of Ms Smith's ring." Other rustlings and murmurs quieted again as Gary Smith, a tear shimmering diamond-bright in the corner of his eye, proudly stepped out with his daughter on his arm, the proudest of proud fathers.

Sienna, a picture of bridal elegance in her bustled and beribboned Edwardian gown, had eyes for no-one except the bearded groom waiting for her at the altar. Whole and free, head up, she advanced proudly to his side. And Joseph Lambert, with eyes for no-one except Sienna, the bride of his dreams, watched her, proud as Punch, every inch of the way till he received her hand from her father.

Hands clasped, lost in a world of their own where love reigned supreme, Reverend Charles had to clear his throat a second time before his blushing bride and groom were ready to proceed.

THE END

If you enjoyed reading

The Making of Joey Lambert, **which I do hope you did, please consider leaving a review on Amazon or Goodreads**

as good reviews are a lovely way for readers to connect with writers. They are also useful in promoting further sales of our books.

Here is Your Preview of
Healing Dr Murphy

An Oxley Crossing Romance,
Book 7 in the series

LENA WEST

1

Unsmiling, Kat Murphy cast her eyes round the reception area, ending her survey by returning her attention to the woman in front of her.

"The old place has changed a lot," she commented in a vain attempt to distract herself from the churning in her gut at what awaited her. "You and your husband," an assumption based on the sign outside stating P & M Morris to be the licensees, and the woman's nametag reading Marge Morris, "have really put some work in."

"Oh," Marge bridled, her broad smile proclaiming her pride. "It was a real work of love. Operating a hotel like this was our dream, and when we saw *The Victoria* we couldn't resist. Oxley Crossing is such a wonderful town. So much history. Have you been here before, then?"

"Umm. A lifetime ago. Before your time. *The Victoria* was a dump back then. I'd like to book a room please. Not sure how long, but possibly a few nights."

Very few, hopefully. Depending how long it takes me to fulfil my Godforsaken mission and shake the dust of The Crossing off my boots. Again. Forever.

Suddenly all business, Marge brought out the guest register.

"If you'll just sign here, I'll take you up to your room. When you've settled in, feel free to take a look around. We've turned the dining room into a museum space with old photos and such. You might find it interesting since you're familiar with The Crossing." Marge Morris turned the guest register of *The Victoria Inn*, Oxley Crossing's historic iron-lace clad hotel, towards her guest.

Familiar with The Crossing! Kat grimaced. *An understatement if ever there was one.*

"My dear!" Marge, idly reading the name in the register, K M Murphy, gasped. "I'm so sorry. Rattling on here about the hotel when you must be in a hurry to get to St Catherine's for the funeral." Now she knew the woman who appeared to be in her early thirties was family, she could easily discern a familial likeness to Colin Murphy in her short, blond hair and bright blue eyes. All the Murphy's had those eyes. Irish eyes, Marge called them.

"Funeral?" A chill tiptoed up Kat's spine. "Who died?"

Please God, not Bridget. Or Pat or Sean.

"You mean you don't know? But I thought … Your name. Murphy. Colin and Therese were killed Friday night when their car ran off the road and hit a tree. Oh, dear. I feel dreadful being the one to tell you this. Were they close relatives?"

Unsure what the sinking feeling in her gut portended, Kat took a moment to assimilate the information.

"That was Colin Murphy? Father of Bridget, Patrick and Sean?"

"Yes," Marge nodded, looking distressed. "And the little ones."

"My father." Kat suppressed the urge to curse. Typical of the Old Bastard. She'd finally decided to mend fences and he upped and died on her. Not knowing who in Hell Therese and the 'little ones' were, she ignored Marge's references to them. "I've just returned from America. I've been out of touch, so no-one was able to reach me. You say the funeral's today?"

Marge, who'd noticed the twang in her guest's speech, nodded again.

No getting out of it. She was here. She'd have to put in an appearance. Although their father's funeral was the last place Kat would have chosen to make her peace with Bridget and the boys.

"What time?"

"This is dreadful! Dreadful!" Wringing her hands, Marge pulled herself together. She wished Phil was here, but he'd just headed round to the church himself. She was only here as she hated funerals and never attended one if she could avoid it. "This is a terrible homecoming for you, Dear. I'm so sorry. You'll have to hurry. The funeral's at ten."

The grandfather clock down the hall obligingly chimed a quarter to. A fatalistic glance at her well-worn Texan cowboy boots, dark jeans and bottle-green leather bomber jacket over a white tailored linen shirt assured Kat, that while she wasn't really dressed appropriately, she'd pass muster in a crowd.

"Look, Marge. Can I leave this bag with you? St Catherine's, you said?"

Marge nodded her head, her directions unheard as Kat strode out, keys in hand to get back behind the wheel. Eighteen years living in The Crossing, fronting up for Mass at St Catherine's Catholic Church every Sunday morning meant she'd have no trouble finding her way.

~~~~~

"We are gathered here today …"

The priest, a stranger, not old Father Ahearn of the Hellfire and Brimstone sermons she'd hated, began the service as Kat entered the church. Dipping her fingers in the Holy Water she made the sign of the Cross. Genuflecting, she was about to slip into a space in the back pew, when she rebelled.

Damn it all! I'm his daughter! I've got the right to sit up front, not cringing away in the back as if I've got something to be ashamed of.

Moving across to the side aisle, she made her way silently forward, wondering who all the people on the front pews were. There were certainly more than she could account for when she performed a mental roll-call. Slipping in beside a dark-suited man, she sat at the very end of the pew.

He turned to see who the late-comer was, his jaw dropping as he recognised her. Now she could see his face, Kat recognised him, too.

"Bloody Hell, Kat. Where'd you spring from?"

"Later Sean." She nudged his elbow, deliberately turning to face the priest who frowned at their disturbance, slight though it was.
~~~~~

Later.

After the church service, thankfully the short version, not the full Mass Kat didn't think she could have sat through, the family led the exodus, following the two sealed coffins out the door.

While most of the congregation headed straight for their cars to drive the short distance to the cemetery on the outskirts of town, a few of the older women who'd recognised the stranger on the family pew as the long-lost Kathleen Murphy, tried to nose their way in to hear her story. They didn't stand a chance. If there was one thing Murphy's were born knowing, it was how to close ranks against outsiders. One icy glare from Bridget, now the senior member of the clan, and they backed off.

With children, teenagers, and a couple of adults Kat took to be in-laws forming a shield-wall around them, Bridget, Patrick and Sean confronted their sister Kathleen.

"Picked your time for the grand homecoming, didn't you, Kat? If you're hoping for rich pickings, hope on. Dad died as he lived, with empty pockets. There's no money for this shindig, let alone anything else, so be prepared to kick in your share."

"Yeah, Sis." Patrick took over from Bridget. "With you here we can split the costs four ways instead of three."

Silence reigned as they waited for her response. The Kathleen they remembered would have jumped in, boots and all, defending herself against her siblings' impugned slur.

Kat shrugged, unable to fault her older siblings' opening topic. They probably had no more idea what to say than she did, and in the Murphy family money had always been vitally important.

Probably because it had been largely non-existent. Still, it looked as if she could forget the fatted calf.

"Naturally I'll pay my share."

Not sure what else she ought to say, Kat played for time. Turning to Sean, she delicately raised a brow, but he, always the quiet one, simply smiled and pretended interest in the clouds gathering to the east behind the ranges. Shrugging again, Kat changed the subject.

"The second coffin. Who was Therese?"

A muffled sob from one of the younger children made her regret her bluntness, but it was too late now.

With a huffing sniff, Bridget, glancing behind her at the gaggle of kids, dropped the hostilities.

"Dad married again, not long after you left, Kat. Therese tried, but in the end, he dragged her down with him. Fill you in later. It's time we made a move to get out to the cemetery before the hearse."

As one, they crossed to the last few cars in the carpark and headed out. Looked as if the Murphy's didn't rate a ceremonial cortege through the town. No big surprise there. The surprise lay in the number of people who'd bothered to turn out. Bringing up the rear, Kat shrugged. It was no use jumping to conclusions with insufficient information. She'd just have to wait for introductions to the horde of new family members who had to be a mish-mash of in-laws, nieces, nephews, and, possibly half-siblings? The 'little ones' Marge had referred to?

~~~~~
~~~~~

Only eight chairs had been set ready in the grave-side front row. Kat, still trailing her siblings, stepped back into the crowd, only to have a burly, grey-haired man in the second row swing his chair into the front and steer her into it. Startled, Kat looked more closely.

"John?" Could this be Bridget's husband? John Hatton? A second, closer look assured her he was. "Thanks."

Once again, the officiating priest frowned Kat into silence. Mouth thinning, she frowned right back at him. Today was the first time in years she'd set foot in a church, and if this disapproving custodian was typical of modern church-men, she wouldn't be in a hurry to make another foray. Defiantly, she held her head high.

Bored with the drawn-out proceedings, Kat slowly surveyed the crowd. A few sort-of familiar faces she lingered on, then passed over. Fifteen years was a long time, but she was sure she'd identified Eddie Turner and a posse of her supporters. Her eyes tracked further, out to the edge of the gathering, meshing with those of a man staring straight back at her from under the wide brim of a battered Akubra.

Her gut clenched. Her breath solidified in her throat. She was drowning in his eyes, but couldn't tear her gaze away. Who in Hell was he? Why was he staring at her? Anyone else would have politely looked away as soon as she caught their eye, so why didn't he? A cold sweat beaded her brow, but since it was actually rather cool, enough so to make her glad of her leather jacket, it wasn't down to the warmth of the day.

Sean, sitting next to her, joggled her elbow, urging her to her feet to file past the grave and toss in the obligatory handful of dirt.

Distracted, she'd completely missed seeing her father, and the step-mother she'd never met, lowered into their graves. Standing withing the shelter of her family, receiving the commiserations murmured by rote as the assembled mourners paid their respects, Kat boldly looked over her shoulder to where the bothersome man had been standing.

Was still standing.

And, her stomach lurched, a shiver feathering a path up her spine, was still staring at her. As she watched, her new-found brother, Mickey, Bridget had called him in her lightning introductions earlier, ran up to him. He turned to speak to the boy, releasing her from her thrall.

Who in Hell is he?

Kat had very definitely never seen that man before in her life.

If she had, she'd have remembered him! That much she knew for certain.

To get

Healing Dr Murphy

as soon as it's released go to

www.lenawestauthor.com

and make sure that you are signed up for news and release notices!

About the Author

Born in the tropical north, Lena lives close to the sea, although over the years she has lived everywhere from large cities to isolated farms. Her most recent home has a deck overlooking the beautiful Blue Water Wonderland of Port Stephens.

After teaching in Queensland and New South Wales she took early retirement to travel Australia in a motorhome. This idyllic lifestyle lasted several years, during which time she indulged in the creation of story plots and their settings, culminating in the fulfillment of her lifelong ambition to be a writer when she learnt how to self-publish her stories.

Storytelling came naturally - she had been making up stories for her own entertainment all her life, but it wasn't until she began traveling that she had time to write down some of her favourites. As well as a series of rural romances set in the fictional town of Oxley Crossing, she writes contemporary romances and Australian historical romances.

With an addiction to happily-ever-afters, in both her reading and her own stories, the romance genre is a natural fit, and the variety of places she has lived have all contributed to the settings in which she brings love to life.

You can find Lena on Facebook at:

https://www.facebook.com/LenaWestAuthor/

or sign up for her newsletter at:

www.lenawestauthor.com

Other Books by

Lena West

Historical Romances

 **Unto Death**

In Colonial society of the 1860s marriage is a contract unto death; and scandal is death of another kind.

https://www.amazon.com/dp/B07D3MZ1L4

____

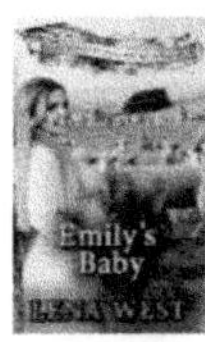 **Emily's baby**

In the 1950s an unwed mother needed help if she was to keep her child. Emily had no family, and no money, but she would do whatever it took to keep her precious baby.

https://www.amazon.com/dp/B07TPDN13W

Contemporary Romances

 **Loving Fenella**

When artist and teacher, Fenella Wilkins, is inspired to paint Greg Kendall, she falls in love with both him and his daughter, Aimee. But he is engaged to the beautiful model, Linda Beck. It is against Fen's principles to poach another woman's man, even when self-centred Linda is the other woman.

https://www.amazon.com/dp/B07B3RLS98/

Forgotten

When a soldier returns from the front minus his memory, is he the same man he was when he left? How can Krista be sure which man she really loves?

https://www.amazon.com/dp/B083Y2ZR28

Contemporary Series

Love in Oxley Crossing Series

In the rural town of Oxley Crossing, love is in the air, and romance triumphs, no matter the challenges.

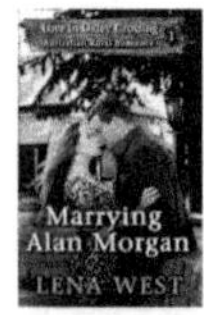

Marrying Alan Morgan

Sparks fly when a feisty red-haired city girl with a past that makes it hard to trust, meets a bitter, disillusioned farmer who's sure love isn't worth the effort. But sometimes, the heart knows better than the mind.

https://www.amazon.com/dp/B0774V1L25/

Saving Jonathon Armitage

A woman come home for family, a man sworn to moving on. Jealousy, distrust and misdirection, are finally resolved, and a life transformed by love.

https://www.amazon.com/dp/B0788GCQJQ

Finding Mr Wright

Escaping her violent ex-husband by claiming sanctuary in Oxley Crossing is the best decision Geni Sullivan has ever made – for herself and her son, nine-year-old Jamie.

https://www.amazon.com/dp/B07C98B7PJ

Electing Robert Whitman

At the second wedding in a matter of months, Sophie James is seated next to the man she had a teenage crush on. A single, unattached man to whom she is still very attracted. When she returns to The Crossing to help her mother, she decides to take a chance on him.

https://www.amazon.com/dp/B07KWKLJG6

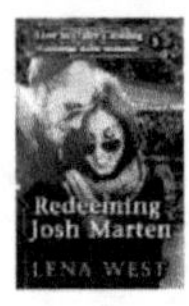

Redeeming Josh Marten

Opposites attract when vibrant, outgoing Thea Benson meets withdrawn, curmudgeonly sculptor, Josh Marten, but behind her bubbly image, Thea is not who she appears to be.

https://www.amazon.com/dp/B07RNHBYG7

The Wyldeflower Series

(Coming soon)

Connect with Lena!

Be the first to know about it when Lena's next book is released!

Sign up to Lena's newsletter at

www.lenawestauthor.com

9 780648 267188